Also by Dorothy Allison
The Women Who Hate Me

STORIES BY

DOROTHY ALLISON

Firebrand
Books
Ithaca, New York

Earlier versions of several of the stories in this book have appeared in *Conditions*, *The Lesbian Fiction Anthology* (Gay Presses of New York), *off our backs*, *On Our Backs*, and *Out/Look*.

Book and cover design by Betsy Bayley
Typesetting by Bets Ltd.

Printed on acid-free paper in the United States by McNaughton and Gunn

Library of Congress Catalog Number: 88-30175
ISBN 0-932379-52-4 (alk. paper)
ISBN 0-932379-51-6 (pbk.: alk paper)

CONTENTS

PREFACE: DECIDING TO LIVE

There was a day in my life when I decided to live.

After my childhood, after all that long terrible struggle to simply survive, to escape my stepfather, uncles, speeding Pontiacs, broken glass and rotten floorboards, or that inevitable death by misadventure that claimed so many of my cousins; after watching so many die around me, I had not imagined that I would ever need to make such a choice. I had imagined the hunger for life in me was insatiable, endless, unshakable.

I became an escapee—one of the ones others talked about. I became the one who got away, who got glasses from the Lions Club, a job from Lyndon Johnson's War On Poverty, and finally went to college on a scholarship. There I met the people I had always read about: girls whose fathers loved them—innocently; boys who drove cars they had not stolen; whole armies of the middle and upper classes I had not truly believed to be real; the children to whom I could not help but compare myself. I matched their innocence, their confidence, their capacity to trust, to love, to be generous against the bitterness, the rage, the pure and terrible hatred that consumed me. Like many others who had gone before me, I began to dream longingly of my own death.

I began to court it. Cowardly, traditionally—that is, in the tradition of all those others like me, through drugs and drinking and stubbornly putting myself in the way of other people's violence. Even now, I cannot believe how it was that everything I survived became one more reason to want to die.

But one morning I limped into my mama's kitchen and sat alone at her dining table. I was limping because I had pulled a muscle in my thigh and cracked two ribs in a fight with the woman I thought

I loved. I remember that morning in all its details, the scratches on my wrists from my lover's fingernails, the look on my mama's face while she got ready to go to work—how she tried not to fuss over me, and the way I could not meet her eyes. It was in my mama's face that I saw myself, my mama's silence, for she behaved as if I were only remotely the daughter she had loved and prayed for. She treated me as if I were in a way already dead, or about to die—as unreachable, as dangerous as one of my uncles on a three-day toot. *That* was so humiliating, it broke my pride. My mouth opened to cry out, but then I shut it stubbornly. It was in that moment I made my decision— not actually the decision to live, but the decision not to die on her. I shut my mouth on my grief and my rage and began to pretend as if I would live, as if there were reason enough to fight my way out of the trap I had made for myself—though I had not yet figured out what that reason was.

I limped around tightlipped through the months it took me to find a job in another city and disappear. I took a bus to that city and spoke to no one, signed the papers that made me a low-level government clerk, and wound up sitting in a motel room eating peanut butter sandwiches so I could use the per diem to buy respectable skirts and blouses—the kind of clothes I had not worn since high school. Every evening I would walk the ten blocks from the training classes to the motel where I could draw the heavy drapes around me, open the windows, and sit wrapped around by the tent of those drapes. There I would sit and smoke my hoarded grass.

Part of me knew what I was doing, knew the decision I was making. A much greater part of me could not yet face it. I was trying to make solid my decision to live, but I did not know if I could. I had to change my life, make baby steps into a future I did not trust, and I began by looking first to the ground on which I stood, how I had become the woman I was. By day I played at being what the people who were training me thought I was—a college graduate and a serious worker, a woman settling down to a practical career with the Social Security Administration. I imagined that if I played at it long enough, it might become true, but I felt like an actress in a role for which she was truly not suited. It took all my concentration not to laugh at inappropriate moments and keep my mouth shut when I did not know what to say at all.

There was only one thing I could do that helped me through those weeks. Every evening I sat down with a yellow legal-size pad, writing out the story of my life. I wrote it all: everything I could remember, all the stories I had ever been told, the names, places, images—how the blood had arched up the wall one terrible night that reccurred persistently in my dreams—the dreams themselves, the people in the dreams. My stepfather, my uncles and cousins, my desperate aunts and their more desperate daughters.

I wrote out my memories of the women. My terror and lust for my own kind; the shouts and arguments; the long, slow glances and slower approaches; the way my hands always shook when I would finally touch the flesh I could barely admit I wanted, the way I could never ask for what I wanted, never accept it if they offered. I twisted my fingers and chewed my lips over the subtle and deliberate lies I had told myself and them, the hidden stories of my life that lay in disguise behind the mocking stories I did tell—all the stories of my family, my childhood, and the relentless deadening poverty and shame I had always tried to hide because I knew no one would believe what I could tell them about it.

Writing it all down was purging. Putting those stories on paper took them out of the nightmare realm and made me almost love myself for being able to finally face them. More subtly, it gave me a way to love the people I wrote about—even the ones I had fought with or hated. In that city where I knew no one. I had no money and nothing to fill the evenings except washing out my clothes, reading cheap paperbacks, and trying to understand how I had come to be in that place. I was not the kind of person who could imagine asking for help or talking about my personal business. Nor was I fool enough to think that could be done without risking what little I'd gained. Still, though I knew the danger of revealing too much about my life, I did not imagine anyone reading my rambling, ranting stories. I was writing for myself, trying to shape my life outside my terrors and help-lessness, to make it visible and real in a tangible way, in the way other people's lives seemed real—the lives I read about in books. I had been a child who believed in books, but I had never really found me or mine in print. My family was always made over into carica-tures or flattened into saintlike stock creatures. I never found my lovers in their strength and passion. Outside my mother's stubbornness and my own outraged arrogance, I had never found any reason to believe in myself. But I had the idea that I could make it exist on those pages.

Days, I went to training sessions, memorized codes, section num-bers, and memo formats. Nights, I wrote my stories. I would pull out scraps of paper at work to make notes about things I wanted to write about, though most of those scraps just wound up tucked in my yellow pad. What poured out of me could not be planned or controlled; it came up like water under pressure at its own pace, pushing my fear ahead of it. By the end of the month, I'd taken to sitting on the motel roof—no longer stoned, but still writing. By then I was also writing letters to all the women I didn't really expect to see again, explaining the things that writing out my stories had made real to me. I did not intend to mail those letters, and never did. The letters themselves were stories—mostly lies—self-justifying, awkward, and desperate.

I finished that month, got assigned to a distant city, put away my yellow papers, and moved—making sure no one who knew me from before could find me. I threw myself into the women's community, fell in love every third day, and started trying to be serious about writing—poems and essays and the beginnings of stories. I even helped edit a feminist magazine. Throughout that time I *told* stories—mostly true stories about myself and my family and my lovers in a drawl that made them all funnier than they were. Though that was mostly a good time for me, I wrote nothing that struck me as worth the trouble of actually keeping. I did not tuck those new stories away with the yellow pads I had sealed up in a blanket box of my mother's. I told myself the yellow pads were as raw and unworked as I felt myself to be, and the funny stories I was telling people were better, were the work of someone who was going to be a "real" writer. It was three years before I pulled out those old yellow sheets and read them, and saw how thin and self-serving my funny stories had become.

The stuff on those yellow pads was bitter. I could not recognize myself in that bitchy whiny hateful voice telling over all those horrible violent memories. They were, oddly, the same stories I'd been telling for years, but somehow drastically different. Telling them out loud, I'd made them ironic and playful. The characters became eccentric, fascinating—not the cold-eyed, mean and nasty bastards they were on the yellow pages, the dangerous frightened women and the more dangerous and just as frightened men. I could not stand it, neither the words on the page nor what they told me about myself. My neck and teeth began to ache, and I was not at all sure I really wanted to live with that stuff inside me. But holding onto them, reading them over again, became a part of the process of survival, of deciding once more to live—and clinging to that decision. For me those stories were not distraction or entertainment; they were the stuff of my life, and they were necessary in ways I could barely understand.

Still, I took those stories and wrote them again. I made some of them funny. I made some of them poems. I made the women beautiful, wounded but courageous, while the men disappeared into the background. I put hope in the children and passion in the landscape while my neck ached and tightened, and I found myself wanting nothing so much as a glass of whiskey or a woman's anger to distract me. None of it was worth the pain it caused me. None of it made me or my people real or understandable. None of it told the truth, and every lie I wrote proved to me I wasn't worth my mother's grief at what she thought was my wasted life, or my sister's cold fear of what I might tell other people about them.

I put it all away. I began to live my life as if nothing I did would survive the day in which I did it. I used my grief and hatred to wall off my childhood, my history, my sense of being part of anything greater than myself. I used women and liquor, constant righteous political work, and a series of grimly endured ordeals to convince myself that I had nothing to decide, that I needed nothing more than what other people considered important to sustain me. I worked on a feminist journal. I read political theory, history, psychology, and got a degree in anthropology as if that would quiet the roar in my own head. I watched women love each other, war with each other, and take each other apart while never acknowledging the damage they did—the damage we all did to each other. I went through books and conferences, CR groups and study groups, organizing community actions and pragmatic coalition fronts. I did things I did not understand for reasons I could not begin to explain just to be in motion, to be trying to do something, change something in a world I wanted desperately to make over but could not imagine for myself.

That was all part of deciding to live, though I didn't know it. Just as I did not know that what I needed had to come up from inside me, not be laid over the top of my head. The bitterness with which I had been born, that had been nurtured in me, could not be eased with a lover or a fight or any number of late-night meetings and clumsily written manifestoes. It may never be eased. The decision to live when everything inside and out shouts death is not a matter of moments but of years, and no one has ever told me how you know when it is accomplished.

But a night finally came when I woke up sweaty and angry and afraid I'd never go back to sleep again. All those stories were rising up my throat. Voices were echoing in my neck, laughter behind my ears, and I was terribly, terribly afraid that I was finally as crazy as my kind was supposed to be. But the desire to live was desperate in my belly, and the stories I had hidden all those years were the blood and bone of it. To get it down, to tell it again, to make sense of something—by god just once—to be real in the world, without lies or evasions or sweet-talking nonsense. I got up and wrote a story all the way through. It was one of the stories from the yellow pages, one of the ones I'd rewritten, but it was different again. I wasn't truly me or my mama or my girlfriends, or really any of the people who'd been there, but it had the feel, the shit-kicking anger and grief of my life. It wasn't that whiny voice, but it had the drawl, and it had, too, the joy and pride I sometimes felt in me and mine. It was not biography and yet not lies, and it resonated to the pulse of my sisters' fear and my lovers' teeth-shaking shouts. It began with my broken ribs and my desperate shame, and it ended with all the questions and decisions still waiting—most of all the decision to live.

It was a rough beginning—my own shout of life against death, of shape and substance against silence and confusion. It was most of all my deep abiding desire to live fleshed and strengthened on the page, a way to tell the truth as a kind of magic not cheapened or distorted by a need to please any damn body at all. Without it, I cannot imagine my own life. Without it, I have no way to know who I am.

One time, twice, once in awhile again, I get it right. Once in awhile, I can make the world I know real on the page. I can make the women and men I love breathe out loud in an empty room, the dreams I dare not speak shape up in the smoky darkness of other people's imaginations. Writing these stories is the only way I know to make sure of my ongoing decision to live, to set moment to moment a small piece of stubbornness against an ocean of ignorance and obliteration.

I write stories. I write fiction. I put on the page a third look at what I've seen in life—the condensed and reinvented experience of a cross-eyed working-class lesbian, addicted to violence, language, and hope, who has made the decision to live, is determined to live, on the page and on the street, for me and mine.

RIVER OF NAMES

At a picnic at my aunt's farm, the only time the whole family ever gathered, my sister Billie and I chased chickens into the barn. Billie ran right through the open doors and out again, but I stopped, caught by a shadow moving over me. My cousin, Tommy, eight years old as I was, swung in the sunlight with his face as black as his shoes— the rope around his neck pulled up into the sunlit heights of the barn, fascinating, horrible. Wasn't he running ahead of us? Someone came up behind me. Someone began to scream. My mama took my head in her hands and turned my eyes away.

Jesse and I have been lovers for a year now. She tells me stories about her childhood, about her father going off each day to the university, her mother who made all her dresses, her grandmother who always smelled of dill bread and vanilla. I listen with my mouth open, not believing but wanting, aching for the fairy tale she thinks is everyone's life.

"What did your grandmother smell like?"

I lie to her the way I always do, a lie stolen from a book. "Like lavender," stomach churning over the memory of sour sweat and snuff.

I realize I do not really know what lavender smells like, and I am for a moment afraid she will ask something else, some question that will betray me. But Jesse slides over to hug me, to press her face against my ear, to whisper, "How wonderful to be part of such a large family."

I hug her back and close my eyes. I cannot say a word.

I was born between the older cousins and the younger, born in a pause of babies and therefore outside, always watching. Once, way before Tommy died, I was pushed out on the steps while everyone

stood listening to my Cousin Barbara. Her screams went up and down
in the back of the house. Cousin Cora brought buckets of bloody
rags out to be burned. The other cousins all ran off to catch the sparks
or poke the fire with dogwood sticks. I waited on the porch making
up words to the shouts around me. I did not understand what was
happening. Some of the older cousins obviously did, their strange
expressions broken by stranger laughs. I had seen them helping her
up the stairs while the thick blood ran down her legs. After a while
the blood on the rags was thin, watery, almost pink. Cora threw them
on the fire and stood motionless in the stinking smoke.

Randall went by and said there'd be a baby, a hatched egg to
throw out with the rags, but there wasn't. I watched to see and there
wasn't; nothing but the blood, thinning out desperately while the
house slowed down and grew quiet, hours of cries growing soft and
low, moaning under the smoke. My Aunt Raylene came out on the
porch and almost fell on me, not seeing me, not seeing anything at
all. She beat on the post until there were knuckle-sized dents in the
peeling paint, beat on that post like it could feel, cursing it and herself and every child in the yard, singing up and down, "Goddamn,
goddamn, that girl...no sense...goddamn!"

I've these pictures my mama gave me—stained sepia prints of bare
dirt yards, plank porches, and step after step of children—cousins,
uncles, aunts; mysteries. The mystery is how many no one remembers. I show them to Jesse, not saying who they are, and when she
laughs at the broken teeth, torn overalls, the dirt, I set my teeth at
what I do not want to remember and cannot forget.

We were so many we were without number and, like tadpoles,
if there was one less from time to time, who counted? My maternal
great-grandmother had eleven daughters, seven sons; my grandmother,
six sons, five daughters. Each one made at least six. Some made nine.
Six times six, eleven times nine. They went on like multiplication
tables. They died and were not missed. I come of an enormous family and I cannot tell half their stories. Somehow it was always made
to seem they killed themselves: car wrecks, shotguns, dusty ropes,
screaming, falling out of windows, things inside them. I am the point
of a pyramid, sliding back under the weight of the ones who came
after, and it does not matter that I am the lesbian, the one who will
not have children.

I tell the stories and it comes out funny. I drink bourbon and
make myself drawl, tell all those old funny stories. Someone always

seems to ask me, which one was that? I show the pictures and she says, "Wasn't she the one in the story about the bridge?" I put the pictures away, drink more, and someone always finds them, then says, "Goddamn! How many of you were there anyway?"

I don't answer.

Jesse used to say, "You've got such a fascination with violence. You've got so many terrible stories."

She said it with her smooth mouth, that chin nobody ever slapped, and I love that chin, but when Jesse spoke then, my hands shook and I wanted nothing so much as to tell her terrible stories. So I made a list. I told her: that one went insane—got her little brother with a tire iron; the three of them slit their arms, not the wrists but the bigger veins up near the elbow; she, now *she* strangled the boy she was sleeping with and got sent away; that one drank lye and died laughing soundlessly. In one year I lost eight cousins. It was the year everybody ran away. Four disappeared and were never found. One fell in the river and was drowned. One was run down hitchhiking north. One was shot running through the woods, while Grace, the last one, tried to walk from Greenville to Greer for some reason nobody knew. She fell off the overpass a mile down from the Sears, Roebuck warehouse and lay there for hunger and heat and dying.

Later, sleeping, but not sleeping, I found that my hands were up under Jesse's chin. I rolled away, but I didn't cry. I almost never let myself cry.

Almost always, we were raped, my cousins and I. That was some kind of joke, too.

What's a South Carolina virgin?
'At's a ten-year-old can run fast.

It wasn't funny for me in my mama's bed with my stepfather, not for my cousin, Billie, in the attic with my uncle, nor for Lucille in the woods with another cousin, for Danny with four strangers in a parking lot, or for Pammie who made the papers. Cora read it out loud: "Repeatedly by persons unknown." They stayed unknown since Pammie never spoke again. Perforations, lacerations, contusions, and bruises. I heard all the words, big words, little words, words too terrible to understand. *DEAD BY AN ACT OF MAN.* With the prick still in them, the broom handle, the tree branch, the grease gun...objects, things not to be believed...whiskey bottles, can openers, grass shears, glass, metal, vegetables...not to be believed, not to be believed.

Jesse says, "You've got a gift for words."

"Don't talk," I beg her, "don't talk." And this once, she just holds me, blessedly silent.

I dig out the pictures, stare into the faces. Which one was I? Survivors do hate themselves, I know, over the core of fierce self-love, never understanding, always asking, "Why me and not her, not him?" There is such mystery in it, and I have hated myself as much as I have loved others, hated the simple fact of my own survival. Having survived, am I supposed to say something, do something, be something?

I loved my Cousin Butch. He had this big old head, pale thin hair, and enormous, watery eyes. All the cousins did, though Butch's head was the largest, his hair the palest. I was the dark-headed one. All the rest of the family seemed pale carbons of each other in shades of blond, though later on everybody's hair went brown or red and I didn't stand out so. Butch and I stood out then—I because I was so dark and fast, and he because of that big head and the crazy things he did. Butch used to climb on the back of my Uncle Lucius's truck, open the gas tank and hang his head over, breathe deeply, strangle, gag, vomit, and breathe again. It went so deep, it tingled in your toes. I climbed up after him and tried it myself, but I was too young to hang on long, and I fell heavily to the ground, dizzy and giggling. Butch could hang on, put his hand down into the tank and pull up a cupped palm of gas, breathe deep and laugh. He would climb down roughly, swinging down from the door handle, laughing, staggering, and stinking of gasoline. Someone caught him at it. Someone threw a match. "I'll teach you."

Just like that, gone before you understand.

I wake up in the night screaming, "No, no, I won't!" Dirty water rises in the back of my throat, the liquid language of my own terror and rage. "Hold me. Hold me." Jesse rolls over on me; her hands grip my hipbones tightly.

"I love you. I love you. I'm here," she repeats.

I stare up into her dark eyes, puzzled, afraid. I draw a breath in deeply, smile my bland smile. "Did I fool you?" I laugh, rolling away from her. Jesse punches me playfully, and I catch her hand in the air.

"My love," she whispers, and cups her body against my hip, closes her eyes. I bring my hand up in front of my face and watch the knuckles, the nails as they tremble, tremble. I watch for a long time while she sleeps, warm and still against me.

James went blind. One of the uncles got him in the face with home-brewed alcohol.

Lucille climbed out the front window of Aunt Raylene's house and jumped. They said she jumped. No one said why.

My Uncle Matthew used to beat my Aunt Raylene. The twins, Mark and Luke, swore to stop him, pulled him out in the yard one time, throwing him between them like a loose bag of grain. Uncle Matthew screamed like a pig coming up for slaughter. I got both my sisters in the tool shed for safety, but I hung back to watch. Little Bo came running out of the house, off the porch, feet first into his daddy's arms. Uncle Matthew started swinging him like a scythe, going after the bigger boys, Bo's head thudding their shoulders, their hips. Afterward, Bo crawled around in the dirt, the blood running out of his ears and his tongue hanging out of his mouth, while Mark and Luke finally got their daddy down. It was a long time before I realized that they never told anybody else what had happened to Bo.

Randall tried to teach Lucille and me to wrestle. "Put your hands up." His legs were wide apart, his torso bobbing up and down, his head moving constantly. Then his hand flashed at my face. I threw myself back into the dirt, lay still. He turned to Lucille, not noticing that I didn't get up. He punched at her, laughing. She wrapped her hands around her head, curled over so her knees were up against her throat.

"No, no," he yelled. "Move like her." He turned to me. "Move." He kicked at me. I rocked into a ball, froze.

"No, no!" He kicked me. I grunted, didn't move. He turned to Lucille. "You." Her teeth were chattering but she held herself still, wrapped up tighter than bacon slices.

"You move!" he shouted. Lucille just hugged her head tighter and started to sob.

"Son of a bitch," Randall grumbled, "you two will never be any good."

He walked away. Very slowly we stood up, embarrassed, looked at each other. We knew.

If you fight back, they kill you.

My sister was seven. She was screaming. My stepfather picked her up by her left arm, swung her forward and back. It gave. The arm went around loosely. She just kept screaming. I didn't know you could break it like that.

I was running up the hall. He was right behind me. "Mama! Mama!" His left hand—he was left-handed—closed around my throat, pushed me against the wall, and then he lifted me that way. I kicked, but I couldn't reach him. He was yelling, but there was so much noise in my ears I couldn't hear him.

"Please, Daddy. Please, Daddy. I'll do anything, I promise. Daddy, anything you want. Please, Daddy."

I couldn't have said that. I couldn't talk around that fist at my throat, couldn't breathe. I woke up when I hit the floor. I looked up at him.

"If I live long enough, I'll fucking kill you."

He picked me up by my throat again.

What's wrong with her?
Why's she always following you around?
Nobody really wanted answers.

A full bottle of vodka will kill you when you're nine and the bottle is a quart. It was a third cousin proved that. We learned what that and other things could do. Every year there was something new.

You're growing up.
My big girl.

There was codeine in the cabinet, paregoric for the baby's teeth, whiskey, beer, and wine in the house. Jeanne brought home MDA, PCP, acid; Randall, grass, speed, and mescaline. It all worked to dull things down, to pass the time.

Stealing was a way to pass the time. Things we needed, things we didn't, for the nerve of it, the anger, the need. *You're growing up,* we told each other. But sooner or later, we all got caught. Then it was, *When are you going to learn?*

Caught, nightmares happened. *Razorback desperate,* was the conclusion of the man down at the county farm where Mark and Luke were sent at fifteen. They both got their heads shaved, their earlobes sliced.

What's the matter, kid? Can't you take it?

Caught at sixteen, June was sent to Jessup County Girls' Home where the baby was adopted out and she slashed her wrists on the bedsprings.

Lou got caught at seventeen and held in the station downtown, raped on the floor of the holding tank.

Are you a boy or are you a girl?

On your knees, kid, can you take it?

Caught at eighteen and sent to prison, Jack came back seven years later blank-faced, understanding nothing. He married a quiet girl from out of town, had three babies in four years. Then Jack came home one night from the textile mill, carrying one of those big handles off the high speed spindle machine. He used it to beat them all to death and went back to work in the morning.

Cousin Melvina married at fourteen, had three kids in two and a half years, and welfare took them all away. She ran off with a carnival mechanic, had three more babies before he left her for a motorcycle acrobat. Welfare took those, too. But the next baby was hydrocephalic, a little waterhead they left with her, and the three that followed, even the one she used to hate so—the one she had after she fell off the porch and couldn't remember whose child it was.

"How many children do you have?" I asked her.

"You mean the ones I have, or the ones I had? Four," she told me, "or eleven."

My aunt, the one I was named for, tried to take off for Oklahoma. That was after she'd lost the youngest girl and they told her Bo would never be "right." She packed up biscuits, cold chicken, and Coca-Cola, a lot of loose clothes, Cora and her new baby, Cy, and the four youngest girls. They set off from Greenville in the afternoon, hoping to make Oklahoma by the weekend, but they only got as far as Augusta. The bridge there went out under them.

"An Act of God," my uncle said.

My aunt and Cora crawled out down river, and two of the girls turned up in the weeds, screaming loud enough to be found in the dark. But one of the girls never came up out of that dark water, and Nancy, who had been holding Cy, was found still wrapped around the baby, in the water, under the car.

"An Act of God," my aunt said. "God's got one damn sick sense of humor."

My sister had her baby in a bad year. Before he was born we had talked about it. "Are you afraid?" I asked.

"He'll be fine," she'd replied, not understanding, speaking instead to the other fear. "Don't we have a tradition of bastards?"

He was fine, a classically ugly healthy little boy with that shock of white hair that marked so many of us. But afterward, it was that bad year with my sister down with pleurisy, then cystitis, and no work, no money, having to move back home with my cold-eyed stepfather. I would come home to see her, from the woman I could not admit I'd been with, and take my infinitely fragile nephew and hold him, rocking him, rocking myself.

One night I came home to screaming—the baby, my sister, no one else there. She was standing by the crib, bent over, screaming red-faced. "Shut up! Shut up!" With each word her fist slammed the mattress fanning the baby's ear.

"Don't!" I grabbed her, pulling her back, doing it as gently as I could so I wouldn't break the stitches from her operation. She had her other arm clamped across her abdomen and couldn't fight me at all. She just kept shrieking.

"That little bastard just screams and screams. That little bastard. I'll kill him."

Then the words seeped in and she looked at me while her son kept crying and kicking his feet. By his head the mattress still showed the impact of her fist.

"Oh no," she moaned, "I wasn't going to be like that. I always promised myself." She started to cry, holding her belly and sobbing. "We an't no different. We an't no different."

Jesse wraps her arm around my stomach, presses her belly into my back. I relax against her. "You sure you can't have children?" she asks. "I sure would like to see what your kids would turn out to be like."

I stiffen, say, "I can't have children. I've never wanted children."

"Still," she says, "you're so good with children, so gentle."

I think of all the times my hands have curled into fists, when I have just barely held on. I open my mouth, close it, can't speak. What could I say now? All the times I have not spoken before, all the things I just could not tell her, the shame, the self-hatred, the fear; all of that hangs between us now—a wall I cannot tear down.

I would like to turn around and talk to her, tell her. . ."I've got a dust river in my head, a river of names endlessly repeating. That dirty water rises in me, all those children screaming out their lives in my memory, and I become someone else, someone I have tried so hard not to be."

But I don't say anything, and I know, as surely as I know I will never have a child, that by not speaking I am condemning us, that I cannot go on loving you and hating you for your fairy-tale life, for not asking about what you have no reason to imagine, for that soft-chinned innocence I love.

Jesse puts her hands behind my neck, smiles and says, "You tell the funniest stories."

I put my hands behind her back, feeling the ridges of my knuckles pulsing.

"Yeah," I tell her. "But I lie."

"THE MEANEST WOMAN EVER LEFT TENNESSEE"

My Grandmother Mattie always said my Great-Grandmother Shirley lived too long.

Shirley Wilmer, of the Knoxville County Wilmers, married Tucker Boatwood when she was past nineteen and he was just barely sixteen. Her family had a peanut farm off to the north of Knoxville, a piece of property they split between the five sons. Shirley was the only daughter. Her inheritance was a cedar chest full of embroidered linen and baby clothes that she and her mama had gotten together over the years, that and sixty dollars in silver that her daddy gave her—a fortune in those days. Granny Mattie swore that when Grandma Shirley died those silver coins were still tied in the same cloth in which she'd gotten them.

Two of her children died of the flu after gathering melons on a frosty fall day. People swore you could cure the flu with a bath of hot oil and comfrey, but Shirley wasn't the kind to gather herbs and certainly not the kind to spend her silver on someone who would. She'd never wanted children anyway and hated the way her own body continuously swelled and delivered. She called the children devils and worms and trash, and swore that, like worms, their natural substance was dirt and weeds.

Shirley Boatwood believed herself to be one of the "quality." "The better people," she told her daughters, "know their own. You watch how it goes, you watch how people treat me down at the mill. They can see who I am. It's in the eyes if nothing else." Mattie, the oldest girl, watched the way her mama's lips thinned and tightened, the way her sisters and brothers held their own mouths pinched together so their lips stuck out. Shirley Boatwood was very proud of getting on at the mill and how much she was earning there, as proud of that as she was ashamed that Tucker still worked in the mine.

"A tight mouth," Tucker Boatwood was heard to say, "a tight mouth betrays a tight heart, and a shallow soul." His wife said nothing, but pulled her lips in tighter still, and the next day he found the doors locked against him when he came home from the mine.

"Woman, what do you think you're doing?" He beat on the front door with a swollen dirty right fist. "Woman! Open this door." He spit and shouted and began to kick the base of the door jam. "Kids, do you hear me? Shirley! Woman!"

Inside, Shirley Boatwood sat at her kitchen table sipping hot tea and staring straight ahead. Mattie stood at the sink with her hands flat to the nozzle of the pump. She stood still, unsure of how she could get past her mama to let her father in the door, and absolutely sure that if she tried it, she'd find herself locked out with him before either of them could get inside.

"Put on another kettle," Shirley told her, staring straight ahead and using her right hand to smooth her hair back behind her pristine white collar. "Make me up another cup of tea." Outside, Tucker went on screaming and kicking. Mattie made the tea while the other children sat quietly on the stairs to the second floor. After a while, the shouting let off and Tucker stomped off the porch. Shirley fed the kids sidemeat and grits, then put them all to bed.

When they got up the next morning, Tucker was sitting at the kitchen table drinking cold water and looking like someone had tried to pull out all his hair. He said nothing, but at the end of the week quit his job in the mine and took a position at the JCPenney textile mill.

"A machinist is a higher class of man," Shirley told the children.

Tucker never got the hang of fixing the big bobbin gears. He'd had a fine talent for the winches and pumps at the mine, but the cables and wheels of the spinning machines confused him. After a few weeks he found himself standing in front of a wheeled cart, pulling off full bobbins and popping on empty ones. His ears rang with the noise and his eyes watered from the dust, but Shirley just shrugged. "Mill workers are a better class of people than miners. I never planned to live my life as a miner's wife." Tucker Boatwood took to slipping whiskey into his cold tea, while his blue eyes faded to a pale grey.

The Boatwood children had bad dreams. After supper they were all required to wash again while their mama watched. "That neck don't look clean to me, Bo. You trying to grow mold in those arm-pits, Mattie? Why are you all so dirty and stupid?" The children scrubbed and scrubbed, while Shirley rubbed her neck with one hand and her bulging belly with another. "I'd kill this thing if I could," she muttered. Her five sons and three daughters dreamed often of their mother, dreamed she came in to wash their faces with lye, to cut off the places where their ears stuck out, to tie down their wag-ging tongues and plane down their purplish genitals.

"You won't need this," they dreamed she told them, as she pulled off one piece or another of their flesh. They dreamed and screamed and woke each other in terror. Sometimes, Shirley beat on the stairs with a broom handle to remind them how much she and Tucker need-ed their sleep. She hated the way they cringed away from her. After all, she never hit them. A pinch was enough if you knew how it should be done. But more than their shameful fear of her, she hated the way Mattie would stare back at her and refuse to drop her eyes.

"You think you're something, don't you?" Shirley would push her face right up to her daughter's flushed and sweating cheekbones. "You think God's got his eye on you?" Shirley would pinch the in-side of Mattie's arm and twist her mouth at the girl's stubborn ex-pression. "Wouldn't nobody take an interest in you if you were to birth puppy dogs and turtles—which you might. You might any day now." She beat the foot of each bed with her broomstick until the children squeezed up near the top. "Boatwoods, you're all purelybred Boatwoods. My side of the family don't even want to know you're alive. I'd swear you an't no kin to me at all."

It was true that Shirley's family took no interest in her children. Once a year Shirley would go alone to visit her mother, but neither her parents nor her brothers ever visited them. The only thing the children knew about their grandparents was Shirley's stories about their house, how big and clean it was, how the porch shone with soapstoned wood and baskets of sweet herbs that Grandma Wilmer used in her cooking, how the neighbors admired her mother and looked up to her daddy. By contrast, their father's father, a widower, was nothing but a drunk.

"Vegetables. . .Hell! The man sells whiskey out of that roadside stand, whiskey I tell you, not tomatoes and squash. He just has those runty old tomatoes there to keep the law off."

"Now Shirley, you know that an't true," Tucker always protested.

"I know what's true, Tucker Boatwood, and I won't have these children spared the truth. You want them to grow up like their grand-father? Like those lazy sisters of yours in their dirt-floor cabins? I surely don't. They grow up to live in dirt and I'll renounce them."

"That woman hates her children," the neighbors all said. They did not say that the children hated her back. It was not possible to know what those children thought, so quiet and still they were. They all had the same face, the same pinched features, colorless hair, and nervous hands. Only their eyes varied in shade, from Bo's seawater blue to Mattie's grapeskin hazel. In the warmer weather, they all took on the same shade of deep red-brown tan acquired from staying away from the house as much as they could, and from long hours spent weeding and picking at their mama's direction in a half-dozen farm-ers' fields.

"Money is hard come by," Shirley told them, pocketing eight cents a week on the boys and three on the girls. "Dreams are all that come free, dreams and talk. And that's all lazy people know about. You should see those bent-necks down at the mill, trying to pretend they're working when they're dreaming or talking. Talk about how badly they're used. Trash don't know the meaning of use. Just like you kids." She tucked the pennies in her kerchief and that in her apron. "The way you eat, you'd think you didn't know the cost of boiled rice."

"Two cents a pound."

When Mattie spoke all the other kids dropped their heads, though Bo and Tucker Junior always turned their faces so they could look up from the side. They knew Mattie was crazy, but they worshipped her craziness and suspected that without her they might have all curled up and died.

"You little whore." Shirley gripped the fabric of her apron in twisted fingers. Her voice was an outraged hiss. "You an't worth two cents a night yourself." Mattie's tanned features paled but she kept her mouth closed and her eyes level with her mother's. They stared each other down, while Tucker wiped his forehead and licked dry cracked lips.

"It's got to be supper time," he pleaded, and Shirley nodded slowly into Mattie's face.

"Let the whore cook it."

"Whores and thieves and bastards," she cursed them when she went into labor that last time. She cursed steadily for hours till Tuck-er sent all the kids off to one of his sister's. "I never wanted no man to touch me. I sure never wanted *you* to touch me. You put death and dirt in me every time. Death, you hear me. All I've got out of you is death and mud and worms."

"It's just the pain," the midwife told Tucker, but neither of them really believed that. Tucker believed that this was the time when Shirley told him the whole truth. The midwife did squeeze Tucker's arm once and say, "Do you notice how she don't really scream?"

The baby finally came in two pieces covered in a stinking bloody scum. Tucker borrowed a car and wrapped Shirley in three blankets to take her into the county hospital. The midwife wrapped up the baby in flour sacks to carry in, too, but Shirley became hysterical when they tried to put it in the car. They had to put it in the trunk before she would calm down.

"Don't you think I knew it was dead?" Shirley curled her fist around Tucker's wrist so tight he thought the little bones would crack. "I told you. You put death in me."

"No telling what causes this kind of thing," the doctor told Tucker. "But she's had her last child, that's for sure."

"You've had your last poke at me," Shirley whispered to Tucker when she could finally talk again. "I never wanted it, and if you ever come to me for it again, I'll cut your thing off and feed it to those damn brats you pulled out of me." Tucker said nothing. The doctor had told him he'd have to be very gentle with Shirley for a while, that she was gonna be weak for a good long while.

"You don't know Shirley," Tucker said. "She might be sick, but she an't never gonna be weak."

It was October when the baby was born dead, and Shirley Boatwood didn't go back to work until May. The pennies saved up over the summer were gone by then, as were the canned goods Tucker's sisters had sent over in the fall. By February, half the Boatwood children were wearing strips of sacking tied around their broken shoes. Every morning they'd stand still while Shirley directed Mattie in tying the sacking correctly. It was Bo's birthday, the eleventh of that month, when she caught hold of Mattie's sleeve as she headed for the door with the other children.

"No," she said. "You're thirteen now, no need to waste your time in school. You either, Bo." All the children stood still for a moment, and then Mattie and Bo stepped back and let the others go. It took Shirley half an hour to get herself dressed, shaking off Mattie's hand when she came to help. It took them all another hour to walk the eight blocks together to the mill. Neither Bo nor Mattie spoke. Both of them just kept looking up to their mother with swollen frightened eyes.

Mattie had small quick hands and a terror of the speeding shut-
tles. She kept her lower lip clenched in her teeth while she worked
to untangle bunched and knotted threads. Bo was clumsy and spent
most of his time crawling underneath frames to grease the wheels that
turned the bobbin belts. Sometimes he crawled right under Mattie's
hands and would hiss up at her to get her attention. Both of them
avoided their father. When their mother came back to work in May,
they avoided her too, but that was easier. Shirley had been transferred from the carding room to finishing. Safely separated from the
rest of the mill by a wire and glass wall, Shirley and twenty other
women ran up towels, aprons, and simple skirts from the end runs
of sample fabric bolts.

"You see what I mean?" Shirley's mouth had grown so tight she
seemed to have no lips at all. "Quality always shows, always finds
its place. That foreman knows who I am."

Mattie sucked her gums and thought of the women at the mill
who stepped aside when her mama passed. Everybody said Shirley
Boatwood believed her piss was wine. Everybody said she repeated
things she heard to the foreman on the second shift. And if Shirley
Boatwood pissed wine, then there was no doubt that nasty son of
a bitch pissed store-bought whiskey.

"When we grow up..." Bo started whispering every night, and
each child would finish the line in turn.

"I'm gonna move to Texas."

"I an't never gonna eat tripe no more."

"I'm gonna have six little babies and buy them anything they
want."

"Gonna treat them good."

"Gonna tell them how pretty they are."

"Gonna love them, love them."

Sometimes Mattie would let the youngest, Billy, climb up into
her lap. She'd hug and stroke him and quietly sing some gospel songs
for him, making up the words she couldn't remember. "When we grow
up," Bo kept whispering. "When we grow up...."

None of them knew what they might not do. Only Mattie had
an idea that it was possible to do anything at all. Walking to work
every morning, she passed the freight siding where James Gibson pulled
barrels off his father's wagon. The Gibsons ran a lumber business,
and most of the cane syrup shipped out of Greenville went out in
their barrels. If he was there, James stopped and watched her walk
by. Every time he saw her pass, he smiled.

"I've got nine brothers," he told her one time, "and not one sister. Lord, I love to look at pretty girls!"

It was the first time anyone had ever suggested Mattie might be pretty. She started leaving home earlier so she could walk slower past the railway siding. On the mornings when one of the other Gibson boys was there, she felt disappointed. They tended to giggle when they saw her, which always made her wonder what James said about her to them.

"I told them to keep an eye on you," James told her when she asked. "I told them to keep their hands off and their eyes open. What you think about that?"

"I think you talking a lot for nothing having been said between us."

"What do we need to say?"

But Mattie couldn't answer that. She didn't know what she wanted to say to anybody. She only knew she wanted to start finding out. She felt as if her eyes were opening, as if light were coming into a dark place inside her. At the dinner table Mattie watched her mama spoon rice out of the bowl, all the while talking about how only trash served food out of a cooking pot.

"Quality people use serving dishes." She slapped Bo's hand. "Quality people don't come to the table with grease under their nails."

"I washed!"

Mattie watched rice grains fall off her fork. She hated butter beans with rice. White on white didn't suit her. Black-eyed peas with pork was better. Best was deep-brown pinto beans cooked soft and thick.

"If you'd really washed, you'd be clean. Nobody in my family ever came to the table with dirt under their nails. You go wash again."

Bo's face creased and uncreased, as if the words he wasn't saying were pushing up inside him. But he kept quiet and went out to the porch to wash again. His father slapped his behind lightly as he went past. Mattie put her fork between her teeth, realizing how bad their father was looking. He wasn't eating nothing either, didn't seem as if he ever ate much anymore, though he drank lots of tea out of his special jar from under the pump.

He's a drunk, Mattie thought, examining the broken veins in her father's nose. He really is a drunk.

"What are you thinking about, Miss High and Mighty?" Shirley spooned butter beans onto another plate and pursed her lips at Mattie.

"Nothing." Mattie filled her mouth with rice so she wouldn't have to talk.

"You got a lot in that face for nothing to say. Mabel Moseley told me she saw you out behind the mill talking to that Gibson boy day before yesterday. She said you were shaking your ass and swinging your hair like some kind of harlot."

Mattie scooped up more rice so that her cheeks bulged out. She looked back at her mother steadily, seeing for the first time not only the thin lips but the corded neck muscles and high red spots on the cheeks. She's pretty ugly, Mattie thought. She let her eyes wander up to her mother's, to the hazel color that reflected her own. You're ugly and old, she thought to herself, but went on chewing steadily.

"Now woman," Tucker pushed his plate forward out of his way. "You know Mabel Moseley an't quite right in her head. Mattie Lee's a good girl . . ."

"She's trash. She's nothing but trash, and you know it." Calmly, Shirley Boatwood set the plate down in front of her youngest and started to fill another plate for herself. "Don't matter what I do, I can't make nothing out of these kids. Seems like they're all bound to grow up to be trash."

Tucker closed his eyes and sighed. "I'm tired," he whispered. "I'm gonna lay me down for a while."

"An't no food gonna be kept warm for you."

"Don't want it no way."

Mattie spooned more rice into her mouth. She watched her mother watching her father as he walked away, shuffling his feet on the floorboards. There were gaps between most of the floorboards, and Shirley was always stuffing them with one thing or the other. What would it be like, Mattie wondered, to live in a house with dirt floors?

"You hear about that union man?" she heard herself say, and her heart seemed to pause briefly in shock.

Her mama was looking at her again. Her mama's mouth was hanging open. Past her shoulder, Bo had stopped in the doorway, wiping his hands on his overalls. "Union?"

"Trade union." Mattie filled her fork again and then looked past her mama to Bo. "You think we ought to sign up, Bo?"

Bo's mouth fell open. "Uh." He stopped and looked from his mama to Mattie to the curtain swaying at the door to the back bedroom where his father had just gone.

"You've gone crazy." Shirley dropped the spoon into the beans. "You've gone absolutely crazy. There an't no union in the mill. There an't gonna be no union in the mill. And I wouldn't let you join one if some fool was to try to bring one in."

"You couldn't stop me."

It felt to Mattie as if the rice was swelling inside her. There was a kind of heat in her belly that was spreading down her legs and tingling. Once she had sipped at her Daddy's tea glass and felt the same thing. "You're drunk, little girl," he'd told her, and she'd kind of liked the feeling. She liked it even more now. She watched her mama's hands flatten on the table. She watched the little red spots in her mama's face get bigger. She watched Bo's eyes widen and a little gleam of light come on in them. There was a kind of laugh in her belly that wanted to roll out her mouth, but she held it in. She imagined Bo's chorus of *when we grow up* and found herself thinking that when she had kids, she'd sit 'em all down on the dirt floor and tell 'em all to sign with the union. Her mother's chair made a hollow sound on the bare wood floor.

Now, she thought. Now she will get up and come over here and slap me. What will I do then? She took another bite of rice and smiled. What will I do then?

Granny Mattie always said my Great-Grandmother Shirley lived too long. "One hundred and fourteen when she died, and didn't nobody want to wash her body for the burying. Had to hire an undertaker's assistant to pick out something to bury her in. She'd left instructions but didn't nobody want to read 'em. Bo had always swore that when she died, he'd throw a party, but shit, he didn't live to see it and his sons didn't have the guts to do it for him. Only thing he ever managed to do was piss on her porch steps the year before he died, while she sat up there staring over his head, pretending she didn't see his dick or nothing. Anybody ever tells you I'm mean, you tell 'em about your Great-Grandma Shirley, the meanest woman that ever left Tennessee."

MAMA

Above her left ankle my mother has an odd star-shaped scar. It blossoms like a violet above the arch, a purple pucker riding the muscle. When she was a little girl in South Carolina they still bled people in sickness, and they bled her there. I thought she was just telling a story, when she first told me, teasing me or covering up some embarrassing accident she didn't want me to know about. But my aunt supported her.

"It's a miracle she's alive, girl. She was such a sickly child, still a child when she had you, and then there was the way you were born."

"How's that?"

"Assbackward," Aunt Alma was proud to be the first to tell me, and it showed in the excitement in her voice. "Your mama was unconscious for three days after you were born. She'd been fast asleep in the back of your Uncle Lucius's car when they hit that Pontiac right outside the airbase. Your mama went right through the windshield and bounced off the other car. When she woke up three days later, you were already out and named, and all she had was a little scar on her forehead to show what had happened. It was a miracle like they talk about in Bible school, and I know there's something your mama's meant to do because of it."

"Oh yeah," Mama shrugged when I asked her about it. "An't no doubt I'm meant for greater things—bigger biscuits, thicker gravy. What else could God want for someone like me, huh?" She pulled her mouth so tight I could see her teeth pushing her upper lip, but then she looked into my face and let her air out slowly.

"Your aunt is always laying things to God's hand that he wouldn't have interest in doing anyway. What's true is that there was a car accident and you got named before I could say much about it. Ask your aunt why you're named after her, why don't you?"

On my stepfather's birthday I always think of my mother. She sits with her coffee and cigarettes, watches the sun come up before she must leave for work. My mama lives with my stepfather still, though she spent most of my childhood swearing that as soon as she had us up and grown, she'd leave him flat. Instead, we left, my sister and I, and on my stepfather's birthday we neither send presents nor visit. The thing we do—as my sister has told me and as I have told her—is think about Mama. At any moment of the day we know what she will be doing, where she will be, and what she will probably be talking about. We know, not only because her days are as set and predictable as the schedule by which she does the laundry, we know in our bodies. Our mother's body is with us in its details. She is recreated in each of us, strength of bone and the skin curling over the thick flesh the women of our family have always worn.

When I visit Mama, I always look first to her hands and feet to reassure myself. The skin of her hands is transparent—large-veined, wrinkled and bruised—while her feet are soft with the lotions I rubbed into them every other night of my childhood. That was a special thing between my mother and me, the way she'd give herself the care of my hands, lying across the daybed, telling me stories of what she'd served down at the truckstop, who had complained and who tipped specially well, and most important, who had said what and what she'd said back. I would sit at her feet, laughing and nodding and stroking away the tightness in her muscles, watching the way her mouth would pull taut while under her pale eyelids the pulse of her eyes moved like kittens behind a blanket. Sometimes my love for her would choke me, and I would ache to have her open her eyes and see me there, to see how much I loved her. But mostly I kept my eyes on her skin, the fine traceries of the veins and the knotted cords of ligaments, seeing where she was not beautiful and hiding how scared it made me to see her close up, looking so fragile, and too often, so old.

When my mama was twenty-five she already had an old woman's hands, and I feared them. I did not know then what it was that scared me so. I've come to understand since that it was the thought of her growing old, of her dying and leaving me alone. I feared those brown spots, those wrinkles and cracks that lined her wrists, ankles, and the soft shadowed sides of her eyes. I was too young to imagine my own death with anything but an adolescent's high romantic enjoyment; I pretended often enough that I was dying of a wasting disease that would give lots of time for my aunts, uncles, and stepfather to mourn me. But the idea that anything could touch my mother, that anything would dare to hurt her was impossible to bear, and I woke up screaming the one night I dreamed of her death—a dream in which I tried bodily to climb to the throne of a Baptist god and demand her return to me. I thought of my mama like a mountain or a cave, a force of nature, a woman who had saved her own life and mine, and would surely save us both over and over again. The wrinkles in her hands made me think of earthquakes and the lines under her eyes hummed of tidal waves in the night. If she was fragile, if she was human, then so was I, and anything might happen. If she was not the backbone of creation itself, then fear would overtake me. I could not allow that, would not. My child's solution was to try to cure my mother of wrinkles in the hope of saving her from death itself.

Once, when I was about eight and there was no Jergens lotion to be had, I spooned some mayonnaise out to use instead. Mama leaned forward, sniffed, lay back and laughed into her hand.

"If that worked," she told me, still grinning, "I wouldn't have dried up to begin with—all the mayonnaise I've eaten in my life."

"All the mayonnaise you've spread—like the butter of your smile, out there for everybody," my stepfather grumbled. He wanted his evening glass of tea, wanted his feet put up, and maybe his neck rubbed. At a look from Mama, I'd run one errand after another until he was settled with nothing left to complain about. Then I'd go back to Mama. But by that time we'd have to start on dinner, and I wouldn't have any more quiet time with her till a day or two later when I'd rub her feet again.

I never hated my stepfather half as much for the beatings he gave me as for those stolen moments when I could have been holding Mama's feet in my hands. Pulled away from Mama's side to run get him a pillow or change the television channel and forced to stand and wait until he was sure there was nothing else he wanted me to do, I entertained myself with visions of his sudden death. Motorcycle outlaws would come to the door, mistaking him for a Drug Enforcement Officer, and blow his head off with a sawed-off shotgun just like the one my Uncle Bo kept under the front seat in his truck. The lawn mower would explode, cutting him into scattered separate pieces the emergency squad would have to collect in plastic bags. Standing and waiting for his orders while staring at the thin black hairs on his balding head, I would imagine his scalp seen through blood-stained plastic, and smile wide and happy while I thought out how I would tell that one to my sister in our dark room at night, when she would whisper back to me her own version of our private morality play.

When my stepfather beat me I did not think, did not imagine stories of either escape or revenge. When my stepfather beat me I pulled so deeply into myself I lived only in my eyes, my eyes that watched the shower sweat on the bathroom walls, the pipes under the sink, my blood on the porcelain toilet seat, and the buckle of his belt as it moved through the air. My ears were disconnected so I could understand nothing—neither his shouts, my own hoarse shameful strangled pleas, nor my mother's screams from the other side of the door he locked. I would not come back to myself until the beating was ended and the door was opened and I saw my mother's face, her hands shaking as she reached for me. Even then, I would not be able to understand what she was yelling at him, or he was yelling at both of us. Mama would take me into the bedroom and wash my face with a cold rag, wipe my legs and, using the same lotion I had rubbed into her feet, try to soothe my pain. Only when she had stopped crying would my hearing come back, and I would lie still and listen to her voice saying my name—soft and tender, like her hand on my back. There were no stories in my head then, no hatred, only an enormous gratitude to be lying still with her hand on me and, for once, the door locked against him.

Push it down. Don't show it. Don't tell anyone what is really going on. We are not safe, I learned from my mama. There are people in the world who are, but they are not us. Don't show your stuff to anyone. Tell no one that your stepfather beats you. The things that would happen are too terrible to name.

Mama quit working honkytonks to try the mill as soon as she could after her marriage. But a year in the mill was all she could take; the dust in the air got to her too fast. After that there was no choice but to find work in a diner. The tips made all the difference, though she could have made more money if she'd stayed with the honkytonks or managed a slot as a cocktail waitress. There was always more money serving people beer and wine, more still in hard liquor, but she'd have had to go outside Greenville County to do that. Neither she nor her new husband could imagine going that far.

The diner was a good choice anyway, one of the few respectable ones downtown, a place where men took their families on Sunday afternoon. The work left her tired, but not sick to death like the mill, and she liked the people she met there, the tips and the conversation.

"You got a way about you," the manager told her.

"Oh yeah, I'm known for my ways," she laughed, and no one would have known she didn't mean it. Truckers or judges, they all liked my mama. And when they weren't slipping quarters in her pocket, they were bringing her things, souvenirs or friendship cards, once or twice a ring. Mama smiled, joked, slapped ass, and firmly passed back anything that looked like a down payment on something she didn't want to sell. She started taking me to work with her when I was still too short to see over the counter, letting me sit up there to watch her some, and tucking me away in the car when I got cold or sleepy.

"That's my girl," she'd brag. "Four years old and reads the funny papers to me every Sunday morning. She's something, an't she?"

"Something," the men would nod, mostly not even looking at me, but agreeing with anything just to win Mama's smile. I'd watch them closely, the wallets they pulled out of their back pockets, the rough patches on their forearms and scratches on their chins. Poor men, they didn't have much more than we did, but they could buy my mama's time with a cup of coffee and a nickel slipped under the saucer. I hated them, each and every one.

My stepfather was a truck driver—a little man with a big rig and a bigger rage. He kept losing jobs when he lost his temper. Somebody would say something, some joke, some little thing, and my little stepfather would pick up something half again his weight and try to murder whoever had dared to say that thing. "Don't make him angry," people always said about him. "Don't make him angry," my mama was always saying to us.

I tried not to make him angry. I ran his errands. I listened to him talk, standing still on one leg and then the other, keeping my face empty, impartial. He always wanted me to wait on him. When we heard him yell, my sister's face would break like a pool of water struck with a handful of stones. Her glance would fly to mine. I would stare at her, hate her, hate myself. She would stare at me, hate me, hate herself. After a moment, I would sigh—five, six, seven, eight years old, sighing like an old lady—tell her to stay there, get up and go to him. Go to stand still for him, his hands, his big hands on his little body. I would imagine those hands cut off by marauders sweeping down on great black horses, swords like lightning bolts in the hands of armored women who wouldn't even know my name but would kill him anyway. Imagine boils and blisters and wasting diseases; sudden overturned cars and spreading gasoline. Imagine vengeance. Imagine justice. What is the difference anyway when both are only stories in your head? In the everyday reality you stand still. I stood still. Bent over. Laid down.

"Yes, Daddy."

"No, Daddy."

"I'm sorry, Daddy."

"Don't do that, Daddy."

"Please, Daddy."

Push it down. Don't show it. Don't tell anyone what is really going on. We are not safe. There are people in the world who are, but they are not us. Don't show your fear to anyone. The things that would happen are too terrible to name.

Sometimes I wake in the middle of the night to the call of my name shouted in my mama's voice, rising from silence like an echo caught in the folds of my brain. It is her hard voice I hear, not the soft one she used when she held me tight, the hard voice she used on bill collectors and process servers. Sometimes her laugh comes too, that sad laugh, thin and foreshadowing a cough, with her angry laugh following. I hate that laugh, hate the sound of it in the night following on my name like shame. When I hear myself laugh like that, I always start to curse, to echo what I know was the stronger force in my mama's life.

As I grew up my teachers warned me to clean up my language, and my lovers became impatient with the things I said. Sugar and honey, my teachers reminded me when I sprinkled my sentences with the vinegar of my mama's rage—as if I was supposed to want to draw flies. And, "Oh honey," my girlfriends would whisper, "do you have to talk that way?" I did, I did indeed. I smiled them my mama's smile and played for them my mama's words while they tightened up and pulled back, seeing me for someone they had not imagined before. They didn't shout, they hissed; and even when they got angry, their language never quite rose up out of them the way my mama's rage would fly.

"Must you? Must you?" they begged me. And then, "For God's sake!"

"Sweet Jesus!" I'd shout back but they didn't know enough to laugh.

"Must you? Must you?"

Hiss, hiss.

"For God's sake, do you have to end everything with *ass*? An anal obsession, that's what you've got, a goddamn anal obsession!"

"I do, I do," I told them, "and you don't even know how to say *goddamn*. A woman who says *goddamn* as soft as you do isn't worth the price of a meal of shit!"

Coarse, crude, rude words, and ruder gestures—Mama knew them all. *You assfucker, get out of my yard*, to the cop who came to take the furniture. *Shitsucking bastard!* to the man who put his hand under her skirt. *Jesus shit a brick*, every day of her life. Though she slapped me when I used them, my mama taught me the power of nasty words. Say *goddamn*. Say anything but begin it with *Jesus* and end it with *shit*. Add that laugh, the one that disguises your broken heart. Oh, never show your broken heart! Make them think you don't have one instead.

"If people are going to kick you, don't just lie there. Shout back at them."

"Yes, Mama."

Language then, and tone, and cadence. Make me mad, and I'll curse you to the seventh generation in my mama's voice. But you have to work to get me mad. I measure my anger against my mama's rages and her insistence that most people aren't even worth your time. "We are another people. Our like isn't seen on the earth that often," my mama told me, and I knew what she meant. I know the value of the hard asses of this world. And I am my mama's daughter—tougher than kudzu, meaner than all the ass-kicking, bad-assed, cold-assed, saggy-assed fuckers I have ever known. But it's true that sometimes I talk that way just to remember my mother, the survivor, the endurer, but the one who could not always keep quiet about it.

We are just like her, my sister and I. That March when my sister called, I thought for a moment it was my mama's voice. The accent was right, and the language—the slow drag of matter-of-fact words and thoughts, but the beaten-down quality wasn't Mama, couldn't have been. For a moment I felt as if my hands were gripping old and tender flesh, the skin gone thin from age and wear, my granny's hands, perhaps, on the day she had stared out at her grandsons and laughed lightly, insisting I take a good look at them. "See, see how the blood thins out." She spit to the side and clamped a hand down on my shoulder. I turned and looked at her hand, that hand as strong as heavy cord rolled back on itself, my bare shoulder under her hand and the muscles there rising like bubbles in cold milk. I had felt thick and strong beside her, thick and strong and sure of myself in a way I have not felt since. That March when my sister called I felt old; my hands felt wiry and worn, and my blood seemed hot and thin as it rushed through my veins.

My sister's voice sounded hollow; her words vibrated over the phone as if they had iron edges. My tongue locked to my teeth, and ·I tasted the fear I thought I had put far behind me.

"They're doing everything they can—surgery again this morning and chemotherapy and radiation. He's a doctor, so he knows, but Jesus..."

"Jesus shit."

"Yeah."

Mama woke up alone with her rage, her grief. "Just what I'd always expected," she told me later. "You think you know what's going on, what to expect. You relax a minute and that's when it happens. Life turns around and kicks you in the butt."

Lying there, she knew they had finally gotten her, the *they* that had been dogging her all her life, waiting for the chance to rob her of all her tomorrows. Now they had her, her body pinned down under bandages and tubes and sheets that felt like molten lead. She had not really believed it possible. She tried to pull her hands up to her neck, but she couldn't move her arms. "I was so mad I wanted to kick holes in the sheets, but there wasn't no use in that." When my stepfather came in to sit and whistle his sobs beside the bed, she took long breaths and held her face tight and still. She became all eyes, watching everything from a place far off inside herself.

"Never want what you cannot have," she'd always told me. It was her rule for survival, and she grabbed hold of it again. She turned her head away from what she could not change and started adjusting herself to her new status. She was going to have to figure out how to sew herself up one of those breast forms so she could wear a bra. "Damn things probably cost a fortune," she told me when I came to sit beside her. I nodded slowly. I didn't let her see how afraid

I was, or how uncertain, or even how angry. I showed her my pride in her courage and my faith in her strength. But underneath I wanted her to be angry, too. "I'll make do," she whispered, showing me nothing, and I just nodded.

"Everything's going to be all right," I told her.

"Everything's going to be all right," she told me. The pretense was sometimes the only thing we had to give each other.

When it's your mama and it's an accomplished fact, you can't talk politics into her bleeding. You can't quote from last month's article about how a partial mastectomy is just as effective. You can't talk about patriarchy or class or confrontation strategies. I made jokes on the telephone, wrote letters full of healthy recipes and vitamin therapies. I pretended for her sake and my own that nothing was going to happen, that cancer is an everyday occurrence (and it is) and death is not part of the scenario.

Push it down. Don't show it. Don't tell anybody what is really going on. My mama makes do when the whole world cries out for things to stop, to fall apart, just once for all of us to let our anger show. My mama clamps her teeth, laughs her bitter laugh, and does whatever she thinks she has to do with no help, thank you, from people who only want to see her wanting something she can't have anyway.

Five, ten, twenty years—my mama has had cancer for twenty years. "That doctor, the one in Tampa in '71, the one told me I was gonna die, that sucker choked himself on a turkey bone. People that said what a sad thing it was—me having cancer, and surely meant to die— hell, those people been run over by pickups and dropped down dead with one thing and another, while me, I just go on. It's something, an't it?"

It's something. Piece by piece, my mother is being stolen from me. After the hysterectomy, the first mastectomy, another five years later, her teeth that were easier to give up than to keep, the little toes that calcified from too many years working waitress in bad shoes, hair and fingernails that drop off after every bout of chemotherapy, my mama is less and less the mountain, more and more the cave—the empty place from which things have been removed.

"With what they've taken off me, off Granny, and your Aunt Grace—shit, you could almost make another person."

A woman, a garbage creation, an assembly of parts. When I drink

I see her rising like bats out of deep caverns, a gossamer woman—all black edges, with a chrome uterus and molded glass fingers, plastic wire rib cage and red unblinking eyes. My mama, my grandmother, my aunts, my sister and me—every part of us that can be taken has been.

"Flesh and blood needs flesh and blood," my mama sang for me once, and laughing added, "but we don't need as much of it as we used to, huh?"

When Mama talked, I listened. I believed it was the truth she was telling me. I watched her face as much as I listened to her words. She had a way of dropping her head and covering her bad teeth with her palm. I'd say, "Don't do that." And she'd laugh at how serious I was. When she laughed with me, that shadow, so grey under her eyes, lightened, and I felt for a moment—powerful, important, never so important as when I could make her laugh.

I wanted to grow up to do the poor-kid-done-good thing, the Elvis Presley/Ritchie Valens movie, to buy my mama her own house, put a key in her hand and say, "It's yours—from here to there and everything in between, these walls, that door, that gate, these locks. You don't ever have to let anyone in that you don't want. You can lay in the sun if you want to or walk out naked in the moonlight if you take the mood. And if you want to go into town to mess around, we can go do it together."

I did not want to be my mother's lover; I wanted more than that. I wanted to rescue her the way we had both wanted her to rescue me. *Do not want what you cannot have*, she told me. But I was not as good as she was. I wanted that dream. I've never stopped wanting it.

The day I left home my stepfather disappeared. I scoured him out of my life, exorcising every movement or phrase in which I recognized his touch. All he left behind was a voice on a telephone line, a voice that sometimes answered when I called home. But Mama grew into my body like an extra layer of warm protective fat, closing me around. My muscles hug my bones in just the way hers do, and when I turn my face, I have that same bulldog angry glare I was always ashamed to see on her. But my legs are strong, and I do not stoop the way she does; I did not work waitress for thirty years, and my first lover taught me the importance of buying good shoes. I've got Mama's habit of dropping my head, her quick angers, and that same belly-gutted scar she was so careful to hide. But nothing marks me so much her daughter as my hands—the way they are aging, the veins coming up through skin already thin. I tell myself they are beautiful as they recreate my mama's flesh in mine.

My lovers laugh at me and say, "Every tenth word with you is *mama*. Mama said. Mama used to say. My mama didn't raise no fool."

I widen my mouth around my drawl and show my mama's lost teeth in my smile.

Watching my mama I learned some lessons too well. Never show that you care, Mama taught me, and never want something you cannot have. Never give anyone the satisfaction of denying you something you need, and for that, what you have to do is learn to need nothing. Starve the wanting part of you. In time I understood my mama to be a kind of Zen Baptist—rooting desire out of her own heart as ruthlessly as any mountaintop ascetic. The lessons Mama taught me, like the lessons of Buddha, were not a matter of degree but of despair. My mama's philosophy was bitter and thin. She didn't give a damn if she was ever born again, she just didn't want to be born again poor and wanting.

I am my mama's daughter, her shadow on the earth, the blood thinned down a little so that I am not as powerful as she, as immune to want and desire. I am not a mountain or a cave, a force of nature or a power on the earth, but I have her talent for not seeing what I cannot stand to face. I make sure that I do not want what I do not think I can have, and I keep clearly in mind what it is I cannot have. I roll in the night all the stories I never told her, cannot tell her still— her voice in my brain echoing love and despair and grief and rage. When, in the night, she hears me call her name, it is not really me she hears, it is the me I constructed for her—the one who does not need her too much, the one whose heart is not too tender, whose insides are iron and silver, whose dreams are cold ice and slate—who needs nothing, nothing. I keep in mind the image of a closed door, Mama weeping on the other side. She could not rescue me. I cannot rescue her. Sometimes I cannot even reach across the wall that separates us.

On my stepfather's birthday I make coffee and bake bread pudding with bourbon sauce. I invite friends over, tell outrageous stories, and use horrible words. I scratch my scars and hug my lover, thinking about Mama twelve states away. My accent comes back and my weight settles down lower, until the ache in my spine is steady and hot. I remember Mama sitting at the kitchen table in the early morning, tears in her eyes, lying to me and my sister, promising us that the time would come when she would leave him—that as soon as we were older, as soon as there was a little more money put by and things were a little easier—she would go.

I think about her sitting there now, waiting for him to wake up and want his coffee, for the day to start moving around her, things to get so busy she won't have to think. Sometimes, I hate my mama. Sometimes, I hate myself. I see myself in her, and her in me. I see us too clearly sometimes, all the little betrayals that cannot be forgotten or changed.

When Mama calls, I wait a little before speaking.

"Mama," I say, "I knew you would call."

GOSPEL SONG

At nine, I knew exactly who and what I wanted to be. Early every Sunday morning I got up to watch the "Sunrise Gospel Hour" and practice my secret ambition. More than anything in the world I wanted to be a gospel singer—a little girl in a white fringed vest with silver and gold crosses embroidered on the back. I wanted grey-headed ladies to cry as they saw my pink cheeks. I wanted people to moan when they heard the throb in my voice as I sang of the miracle in my life. I wanted a miracle in my life. I wanted to be a gospel singer and be loved by the whole wide world.

All that summer, while Mama was off at work, I haunted the White Horse Cafe over on the highway. They had three Teresa Brewer songs on the jukebox, and the truckers loved Teresa as much as I did. I'd sit out under the jalousie windows and hum along with her, imagining myself crooning with a raw and desperate voice. Half asleep in the sun, reassured by the familiar smell of frying fat, I'd make promises to God. If only He'd let it happen! I knew I'd probably turn to whiskey and rock-and-roll like they all did, but not for years, I promised. Not for years, Lord. Not till I had glorified His Name and bought my mama a yellow Cadillac and a house on Old Henderson Road.

Jesus, make me a gospel singer, I prayed, while Teresa sang of what might have been God and, then again, might have been some black-eyed man. Make me, oh make me! But Jesus must have been busy with Teresa 'cause my voice went high and shrill every time I got excited, and cracked and went hoarse if I tried to croon. The preacher at Bushy Creek Baptist wouldn't even let me stand near the choir to turn the pages of a hymnal. Without a voice like Teresa's or June Carter's, I couldn't sing gospel. I could just listen to it and watch the grey-headed ladies cry. It was an injustice I could not understand or forgive. It left me with a wild aching hunger in my heart and a deep resentment I hid from everyone but God.

My friend Shannon Pearl had the same glint of hunger in her watery pink eyes. An albino, perennially six inches shorter than me, Shannon had white skin, white hair, pale eyes, and fine blue blood vessels showing against the ivory of her scalp. Blue threads under the linen, her mama was always saying. Sometimes Shannon seemed strangely beautiful to me, as she surely was to her mother. Sometimes, but not often. Not often at all. But every chance she could get, Mrs. Pearl would sit her daughter between her knees and purr over that gossamer hair and puffy pale skin.

"My little angel," Mrs. Pearl would croon, and my stomach would push up against my heart.

It was a lesson in the power of love. Looking back at me from between her mother's legs, Shannon was wholly monstrous, a lurching hunched creature shining with sweat and smug satisfaction. There had to be something wrong with me, I was sure, the way I went from awe to disgust where Shannon was concerned. When Shannon sat between her mama's legs or chewed licorice strings her daddy held out for her, I purely hated her. But when other people would look at her hatefully or the boys up at Lee Highway would call her "Lard Eyes," I felt a fierce and protective love for her, as if she were more my sister than Reese. I felt as if I belonged to her in a funny kind of way, as if her "affliction" put me deeply in her debt. It was a mystery, I guessed, a sign of grace like my Catholic Aunt Maybelle was always talking about.

I met Shannon Pearl on the first Monday of school the year I entered the third grade. She got on the bus two stops after Reese and me, walking stolidly past a dozen hooting boys and another dozen flushed and whispering girls. As she made her way up the aisle, I watched each boy slide to the end of his seat to block her sitting with him and every girl flinch away as if whatever Shannon had might be catching. In the seat ahead of us Danny Powell leaned far over into the aisle and began to make retching noises.

"Cootie Train! Cootie Train!" somebody yelled, as the bus lurched into motion and Shannon still hadn't found a seat.

I watched her face—impassive, contemptuous, and stubborn. Sweat was showing on her dress but nothing showed in her face except for the eyes. There was fire in those pink eyes, a deep fire I recognized, banked and raging. Before I knew it I was on my feet and leaning forward to catch her arm. I pulled her into our row without a word. Reese stared at me like I was crazy, but Shannon settled herself and started cleaning her bottleglass lenses as if nothing at all was happening.

I glared at Danny Powell's open mouth until he turned away from us. Reese pulled a strand of her lank blonde hair into her mouth and pretended she was sitting alone. Slowly, the boys sitting near us turned their heads and began to mutter to each other. There was one soft "Cootie Bitch" hissed in my direction, but no yelling. Nobody knew exactly why I had taken a shine to Shannon, but everyone at Greenville Elementary knew me and my family—particularly my matched set of cousins, big unruly boys who would just as soon toss a boy as a penny against the school walls if they heard of an insult against any of us.

Shannon Pearl spent a good five minutes cleaning her glasses and then sat silent for the rest of the ride to school. I understood intuitively that she would not say anything, would in fact generously pretend to have fallen into our seat. I sat there beside her watching the pinched faces of my classmates as they kept looking back toward us. Just the way they stared made me want to start a conversation with Shannon. I imagined us discussing all the enemies we had in common while half the bus craned their necks to try to hear. But I couldn't bring myself to actually do that, couldn't even imagine what to say to her. Not till the bus crossed the railroad tracks at the south corner of Greenville Elementary did I manage to force my mouth open enough to say my name and then Reese's.

She nodded impartially and whispered "Shannon Pearl" before taking off her glasses to begin cleaning them all over again. With her glasses off she half shut her eyes and hunched her shoulders. Much later, I would realize that she cleaned her glasses whenever she needed a quiet moment to regain her composure, or more often, just to put everything around her at a distance. Without glasses, the world became a soft blur, but she also behaved as if the glasses were all that made it possible for her to hear. Commotion or insults made while she was cleaning her glasses never seemed to register at all. It was a valuable trick when you were the object of as much ridicule as Shannon Pearl.

Christian charity, I knew, would have had me smile at Shannon but avoid her like everyone else. It wasn't Christian charity that made me give her my seat on the bus, trade my third-grade picture for hers, sit at her kitchen table while her mama tried another trick on her

wispy hair—*Egg and cornmeal, that'll do the trick. We gonna put curls
in this hair, darling, or my name an't Roseanne Pearl*—or follow her to
the Bushy Creek Highway Store and share the blue popsicle she
bought us. Not Christian charity; my fascination with her felt more
like the restlessness that made me worry the scabs on my ankles. As
disgusting as it all seemed, I couldn't put away the need to scratch
my ankles, or hang around what Granny called "that strange and
ugly child."

Other people had no such problem. Other than her mother and
I, no one could stand Shannon. No amount of Jesus's grace would
make her even marginally acceptable, and people had been known
to suddenly lose their lunch from the sight of the clammy sheen of
her skin, her skull showing blue-white through the thin, colorless
hair and those watery pink eyes flicking back and forth, drifting in
and out of focus.

Lord! But that child is ugly.

It's a trial, Jesus knows, a trial for her poor parents.

They should keep her home.

Now, honey. That's not like you. Remember, the Lord loves a charitable heart.

*I don't care. The Lord didn't intend me to get nauseous in the middle
of Sunday services. That child is a shock to the digestion.*

I had the idea that because she was so ugly on the outside, it
was only reasonable that Shannon would turn out to be saintlike
when you got to know her. That was the way it would have been
in any storybook the local ladies' society would have let me borrow.
I thought of *Little Women, The Bobbsey Twins,* and all those novels
about poor British families at Christmas. Tiny Tim, for Christ's sake!
Shannon, I was sure, would be like that. A patient and gentle soul
had to be hidden behind those pale and sweaty features. She would
be generous, insightful, understanding, and wise beyond her years.
She would be the friend I had always needed.

That she was none of these was something I could never quite
accept. Once she relaxed with me, Shannon invariably told horrible
stories, most of which were about the gruesome deaths of innocent
children. . . . *And then the tractor backed up over him, cutting his body
in three pieces, but nobody seen it or heard it, you see, 'cause of the noise
the thresher made. So then his mama come out with iced tea for everybody. And she put her foot down right in his little torn open stomach.
And oh Lord! don't you know. . . .*

I couldn't help myself. I'd sit and listen, open-mouthed and fascinated, while this shining creature went on and on about decapitations. She loved best little children who had fallen in the way of large machines. It was something none of the grownups knew a thing about, though once in a while I'd hear a much shorter, much tamer version of one of Shannon's stories from her mama. At those moments, Shannon would give me a grin of smug pride. Can't I tell it better? she seemed to be saying. Gradually I admitted to myself what hid behind Shannon's impassive pink and white features. Shannon Pearl simply and completely hated everyone who had ever hurt her, and spent most of her time brooding on punishments either she or God would visit on them. The fire that burned in her eyes was the fire of outrage. Had she been stronger or smarter, Shannon Pearl would have been dangerous. But half-blind, sickly, and ostracized, she was not much of a threat to anyone.

Shannon's parents were as short as she was, and almost as pale. Mr. and Mrs. Pearl ran a religious supply store downtown south of Main Street, a place where you could get embossed Bibles, bookmarks with the 23rd Psalm in blue relief, hot plates featuring the Sermon on the Mount, and Jesus and that damned lamb on everything imaginable—slipcovers, tablecloths, even plastic pants to go over baby diapers. It seemed a hell of a way for grown people to make a living, and it didn't quite cover Shannon's medical expenses. Mrs. Pearl had to run a sewing service on the side, and Mr. Pearl did bookings for country and gospel singers.

The latter made all the difference in how I felt about the Pearls. Shannon got to meet them: the Blue Ridge Mountain Boys, the Tuckerton Family, the Carter Family, Little Pammie Gleason (blessed by God), the Smoky Mountain Boys, and now and then—every time he'd get saved—Johnny Cash. Sunday morning, Sunday evening, Wednesday prayer service, revival weeks; Mr. Pearl would book a hall, a church or a local TV program. Because Shannon got to go, after a while so did I. I tried to stop worrying about my fascination with the Pearls, crediting it to the more acceptable lust for gospel music.

Driving from Greenville to Greer on Highway 85 past the Sears, Roebuck warehouse, the airbase, the rolling green and red mud hills—a trip we made almost every other day—my stepfather never failed to get us all to sing like some traveling gospel family. *WHILE I WAS SLEEPING SOMEBODY TOUCHED ME, WHILE I WAS SLEEPING, OH! SOMEBODY TOUCHED ME...MUST'HA BEEN THE*

HAND OF THE LORD....

Full voice, all out, late evening gospel music filled the car and shocked the passing traffic. My stepfather never drove fast, and not a one of us could sing worth a damn. My sisters howled and screeched, my mama's voice broke like she, too, dreamed of Teresa Brewer, and my stepfather made sounds that would have scared cows. None of them cared, and I tried not to let it bother me. I'd put my head out the window and howl for all I was worth. The wind filled my mouth and the roar obscured the fact that I sang as badly as any of them. Sometimes at the house I'd even go sing into the electric fan. It made my voice buzz and waver like a slide guitar, an effect I particularly liked, though Mama complained it gave her a headache and would give me an earache if I didn't cut it out.

I took the fan out on the backporch and sang to myself. Maybe I wouldn't get to be the star on the stage, maybe I'd wind up singing background in a "family"—all of us dressed alike in electric blue fringed blouses with silver embroidery. All I needed was a chance to turn my soulful brown eyes on a tent full of believers, sing out the little break in my mournful voice. I knew I could make them love me. There was a secret to it, but I would find it out. If Shannon Pearl could do it to me, I would find a way to do it to the world.

Shannon's mama, Mrs. Pearl, thought I was a precious child.

"Those eyes of yours could break the heart of God," she'd tell me, and pat my black hair fiercely. I'd blink my eyes and try to tear up for her. "Lashes, Bob, look at the lashes on this child. You grow up you can do Maybelline commercials on the television, honey. 'Course not that you're going to want to. You don't ever let anybody talk you into putting any of that junk on you. Your eyes are a gift from GOD!"

Mrs. Pearl had more ways of saying *God* and *Jesus* than any preacher I'd ever heard. She could put it out real soft and low—*gawd*—so that you imagined Him as an uncle in the family, quiet and well-mannered; or drag it out long and loud—GOOOODDDD—a shocking hollow-voiced moan that rocked me like thunder.

Jesus was even better. Everybody said *Jesus* so much, you could forget who and what he was supposed to be, but Mrs. Pearl rationed her *Jesuses*, never failing to give you the sense that Jesus was a real person: a little boy used to bringing doves back to life, a quiet young man never known to curse or fornicate, a man aged by the sin of the world, a life sacrificed for you personally.

It was a bit much to bear at nine, but I expected you got used to it as you got older.

Mrs. Pearl's specialty sewing was the backbone of the Pearl family income. Not surprisingly, she was famous for gilt-rendered scenes on the costumed sleeves and jackets of gospel performers. I got to where I could spot a Mrs. Pearl creation on the Sunrise Gospel Hour without even trying too hard. She had a way of putting little curlicues at the base of the cross that was supposed to suggest grass, but for everyone who knew her, it was an artist's signature.

Mrs. Pearl loved her work. "I feel like my whole life is a joy to the Lord," she'd say, knotting tassels on a red silk blouse for one of the younger Carter girls. "My sewing, Mr. Pearl's work, the store, my precious daughter." She'd glance over at Shannon with a look that mirrored the close-up of Mary and the Baby in the center of the *Illustrated Christian Bible* that was always on special down at the store. "Everything that comes to us is a blessing or a test. That's all you need to know in this life. . . just the certainty that God's got His eye on you, that He knows what you are made of, what you need to grow on. Why questioning's a sin, it's pointless. He will show you in His own good time. And long as I remember that, I'm fine. It's like that song Mr. Pearl likes so much. . . 'Jesus is the engineer, trust his hand on the throttle. . .!' "

Shannon giggled and waved me out on the porch. "Sometimes Mama needs a little hand on her throttle. You know what I mean?" She laughed and rolled her eyes like a broken kewpie doll. "Daddy has to throttle her back down to a human level or she'd take off like a helium angel."

I couldn't help myself. I laughed back, remembering what my Aunt Grace had said about Mrs. Pearl. *If she'd been fucked right just once, she'd have never birthed that weird child.* I poked Shannon on one swollen arm, just in case she could read behind my eyes.

"Your Mama's an an-gel," I whispered hoarsely, mocking the way Mrs. Pearl would say that, "just an an-gel of Ga-ahd."

"Gaa-ad da-am right," Shannon whispered back, and I saw her hatred burning pink and hot in those eyes. It scared and fascinated me. Was it possible she could see the same thing in my eyes? Did I have that much hate in me? I looked back at Mrs. Pearl, humming around the pins in her mouth. A kind of chill went through me. Did I hate Mrs. Pearl? I looked 'round at their porch, the baby's breath hanging in baskets and the two rocking chairs with handsewn cushions. Shannon's teeth flashed sunlight into my eyes.

"You look like the devil's walking on your grave."

I shivered, and then spit like my granny would. "The grave that I'll lie in an't been dug yet." It was something I'd heard Granny say. Shannon grabbed my arm and gave it a jerk.

"Don't say that. It's bad luck to mention your own grave. They say my Grandmother McCray joked about her burying place on Easter morning and fell down dead at evening service." She jerked my arm again hard. "Think about something else quick." I looked down at her hand on my arm, puffy white fingers gripping my thin brown wrist.

"That child will rot fast when she goes," Granny had said once. I felt nauseous.

"I got to go home." Open-mouthed, I pulled air in fast as I could. "Mama wants me to help her hang out the laundry this afternoon."

"Your mama's always making you work."

And yours never does, I thought. I took a deep breath, trying to get my stomach under control. Sometimes I really couldn't stand Shannon Pearl. "We're gonna go to the diner for supper tonight. They have peach cobbler this time of year."

"My daddy's gonna make fresh ice cream tonight." Shannon smiled a smile full of the pride of family position. "We got black walnuts to put on it."

I didn't say anything. She would. She would rot very fast.

There was a circuit that ran from North Carolina to South Carolina, Tennessee, Georgia, Alabama. The gospel singers moved back and forth on it, a tide of gilt and fringed jackets that intersected and paralleled the country western circuit. Sometimes you couldn't tell the difference, and as times got harder certainly Mr. Pearl stopped making distinctions, booking any act that would get him a little cash up front. More and more, I got to go off with the Pearls in their old yellow DeSoto, the trunk stuffed with boxes of religious supplies and Mrs. Pearl's sewing machine, the back seat crowded with Shannon and me and piles of sewing. Pulling into small towns in the afternoon so Mr. Pearl could do the setup and Mrs. Pearl could repair tears and frayed edges of embroidery, Shannon and I would go off to picnic alone on cold chicken and chow-chow. Mrs. Pearl always brought tea in a mason jar, but Shannon would rub her eyes and complain of a headache until her Mama gave in and bought us RC Colas.

Most of the singers arrived late.

It was a wonder to me that the truth never seemed to register with Mr. and Mrs. Pearl. No matter who fell over the boxes backstage, they never caught on that the whole Tuckerton family had to be pointed in the direction of the stage, nor that Little Pammie Gleason—*Lord, just thirteen!*—had to wear her frilly blouse long-sleeved 'cause she had bruises all up and down her arms from that red-headed boy her daddy wouldn't let her marry. They never seemed to see all the "boys" passing bourbon in paper cups backstage or their angel daughter, Shannon, begging for "just a sip." Maybe Jesus shielded their eyes the way he kept old Shadrach, Meshach, and Abednego safe in the fiery furnace. Certainly sin didn't touch them the way it did Shannon and me. Both of us had learned to walk carefully backstage, with all those hands reaching out to stroke our thighs and pinch the nipples we barely had yet.

"Playful boys," Mrs. Pearl would laugh, stitching the sleeves back on their jackets, the rips in their pants. It was a wonder to me that she couldn't smell the whiskey breath set deep in her fine embroidery. But she didn't, and I wasn't gonna commit the sin of telling her what God surely didn't intend her to know.

"Sometimes you'd think Mama's simple," Shannon told me. It was one of those times I was keeping my head down, not wanting to say anything. It was her *mama.* I wouldn't talk about my mama that way even if she was crazy. I wished Shannon would shut up and the music would start. I was still hungry. Mrs. Pearl had packed less food than usual, and Mama had told me I was always to leave something on my plate when I ate with Shannon. I wasn't supposed to make them think they had to feed me. Not that that particular tactic worked. I'd left half a biscuit, and damned if Shannon hadn't popped it in her mouth.

"Maybe it's all that tugging at her throttle." Shannon started giggling funny, and I knew somebody had finally given her a pull at a paper cup. Now, I thought, now her mama will have to see. But when Shannon fell over her sewing machine, Mrs. Pearl just laid her down with a wet rag on her forehead.

"It's the weather," she whispered to me, over Shannon's sodden head. It was so hot, the heat was wilting the pictures off the paper fans provided by the local funeral home. But if there had been snow up to the hubcaps, Mrs. Pearl would have said it was the chill in the air. An hour later, one of the Tuckerton cousins spilled a paper cup on Mrs. Pearl's sleeve, and I saw her take a deep, painful breath. Catching my eye, she just said, "Can't expect that frail soul to cope without a little help."

I didn't tell her that it seemed to me that all those "boys" and "girls" were getting a hell of a lot of "help." I just muttered an almost inaudible *yeah* and cut my sinful eyes at them all.

"We could go sit under the stage," Shannon suggested. "It's real nice under there."

It was nice, close and dark and full of the sound of people stomping on the stage. I put my head back and let the dust drift down on my face enjoying the feeling of being safe and hidden, away from all the people. The music seemed to be vibrating in my bones. *TAK-ING YOUR MEASURE, TAKING YOUR MEASURE, JESUS AND THE HOLY GHOST ARE TAKING YOUR MEASURE....*

I didn't like the new music they were singing. It was a little too gimmicky. *TWO CUPS, THREE CUPS, A TEASPOON OF RIGHT-EOUS. HOW WILL YOU MEASURE WHEN THEY CALL OUT YOUR NAME?* Shannon started laughing. She put her hands around me and rocked her head back and forth. The music was too loud, and I could smell whiskey all around us. My head hurt terribly; the smell of Shannon's hair was making me sick.

"Uh huh uh," I started to gag. Desperately I pushed Shannon away and crawled for the side of the stage as fast as I could. Air, I had to have air.

"Uh huh uh," I rolled out from under the stage and hit the side of the tent. Retching now, I jerked up the side of the tarp and wiggled through. Out in the damp evening air, I just let my head hang down and vomited between my wide, spread hands. Behind me Shannon was gasping and giggling.

"You're sick, you poor baby." I felt her hand on the small of my back pushing down comfortingly.

"Lord God!"

I looked up. A very tall man in a purple shirt was standing in front of me. I dropped my head and puked again. He had silver boots with cracked heels. I watched him step back out of range.

"Lord God!"

"It's all right," Shannon got to her feet beside me, keeping her hand on my back. "She's just a little sick." She paused. "If you got her a Co-Cola, it might settle her stomach."

I wiped my mouth, then wiped my hand on the grass. I looked up. Shannon was standing still, sweat running down into her eyes and making her blink. I could see she was hoping for two cokes. The man was still standing there with his mouth hanging open, a look of horror and shock on his face.

"Lord God," he said again, and I knew before he spoke what he was gonna say. It wasn't me who'd surprised him.

"Child, you are the ugliest thing I have ever seen."

Shannon froze. Her mouth fell open and as I watched, her whole face seemed to cave in. Her eyes shrank to little dots and her mouth became a cup of sorrow. I pushed myself up.

"You bastard!" I staggered forward and he backed up, rocking on his little silver heels. "You goddamned gutless son of a bitch!" His eyes kept moving from my face to Shannon's wilting figure. "You think you so pretty? You ugly sack of shit! You shit-faced turd-eating..."

"SHANNON PEARL!"

Mrs. Pearl was coming 'round the tent.

"You girls...." She gathered Shannon up in her arms. "Where have you been?" The man backed further away. I breathed through my mouth, though I no longer felt so sick. I felt angry and helpless and I was trying hard not to start crying. Mrs. Pearl clucked between her teeth and stroked Shannon's limp hair. "What have you been doing?"

Shannon moaned and buried her face in her mama's dress. Mrs. Pearl turned to me. "What were you saying?" Her eyes glittered in the arc lights from the front of the tent. I wiped my mouth again and said nothing. Mrs. Pearl looked to the man in the purple shirt. The confusion on her face seemed to melt and quickly became a blur of excitement and interest.

"I hope they weren't bothering you," she told him. "Don't you go on next?"

"Uh, yeah." He looked like he wasn't sure. He couldn't take his eyes off Shannon. He shook himself. "You Mrs. Pearl?"

"Why, that's right." Mrs. Pearl's face was glowing.

"I'd heard about you. I just never met your daughter before."

Mrs. Pearl seemed to shiver all over but then catch herself. Pressed to her mama's stomach, Shannon began to wail.

"Shannon, what *are* you going on for?" She pushed her daughter away from her side and pulled out a blue embroidered handkerchief to wipe her face.

"I think we all kind of surprised each other." The man stepped forward and gave Mrs. Pearl a slow smile, but his eyes kept wandering back to Shannon. I wiped my mouth again and stopped myself from spitting. Mrs. Pearl went on stroking her daughter's face but looking up into the man's eyes.

"I love it when you sing," she said, and half giggled. Shannon pulled away from her and stared up at them both. The hate in her face was terrible. For a moment I loved her with all my heart.

"Well," the man said. He rocked from one boot to the other. "Well...."

I reached for Shannon's hand. She slapped mine away. Her face was blazing. I felt as if a great fire was burning close to me, using up all the oxygen, making me pant to catch my breath. I laced the fingers of my hands together and tilted my head back to look up at the stars. If there was a God, then there would be justice. If there was justice, then Shannon and I would someday make them all burn. We walked away from the tent toward Mr. Pearl's battered DeSoto.

"Some day," Shannon whispered.

"Yeah," I whispered back. We knew exactly what we meant.

"Bullshit and applebutter," Granny Mattie laughed later when I told her about it. "Some of these Christian women will believe anything for the sake of a gospel singer."

"Anything." I loved the way she said that. Granny's *Christian women* came out like new spit on a dusty morning, pure and precious and deeply satisfying.

"Anything," I echoed her, and she grinned at me with her toothless, twisted mouth. We were sitting in the backyard close together in Mama's lawn chairs. Granny always complained about Mama not living in houses with porches and rocking chairs, but she liked Mama's reclining lawn chair. Now she reached out, put her hand on the back of my neck, squeezed, and laughed.

"You got a look like your granddaddy sometimes." She pinched me and laughed again. "Bastard was meaner than a snake, but he had his ways. And didn't I love his ways? Lord Christ!" She pulled back and rolled the snuff around in her mouth.

"Man had only two faults I couldn't abide. Wouldn't work to save his life and couldn't stay away from gospel singers. Used to stand out back of revival tents offering 'em the best whiskey made in Greenville county. Then he'd bring me that slush they cleaned out of the taps. Bastard!" She stiffened and looked back over her shoulder, afraid my mama might be behind her. Mama didn't allow anybody to use that word in her house.

"Well, shit," she spit to the side. "You got a little of that too, don't you? A little of that silliness, that revival crap?"

"Aunt Grace says you a heathen."

"Oh Aunt Grace, huh. Aunt Grace fucked her oldest boy."
My mouth fell open. Granny wiped her chin.

"Don't you go telling your mama everything you hear."

"No ma'am."

"And don't go taking that gospel stuff seriously. It's nice to clean you out now and then, but it an't for real. It's like bad whiskey. Run through you fast and leave you with a pain'll lay you down." She wiped her chin again and sighed. I hated that sigh. I liked her better when she was being mean. When she started sighing, she was likely to start crying. Then her face would squeeze down on itself in a way that scared me.

"I an't no fool." I rocked my chair back and forth, pushing off hard with my bare feet. Granny's face twitched, and I saw the light come back into her eyes.

"You know how your mama feels about that word." It was true. Mama had given me one of her rare spankings for calling Reese a fool. She hated it almost as much as *bastard.*

"An't no fool and an't no bastard." I rocked steadily, watching Granny's face.

Granny laughed and looked back over her shoulder nervously. "Oh, you gonna be the death of your mama, and won't I be sorry then?"

She didn't look sorry. She looked better with the lights back in her eyes. I said it again.

"An't no fool and an't no bastard."

Granny started laughing so hard she choked on her snuff.

"You're both, and you just silly 'bout that music just like your granddaddy." She sounded like she was gonna strangle from laughing. "And goddamn, he was both too."

It was a family thing, after all. My Uncle Jack got work building a carport and took some of the money to get Mama a little electric record player and four records. "That's all I'm giving for free," he told her, scooping up gravy with one of her biscuits. "Get you some of those June Carter songs you like. What's that funny one? 'Nickelodeon,' right?"

He scooped and sopped, and drank sweet tea down like it was whiskey. Mama said he'd eaten so many of her biscuits by now, he was like a child of her own.

"A man belongs to the woman that feeds him."

"Bullshit," Aunt Grace insisted. "It's the other way around and you know it. It's the woman belongs to the ones she's got to feed."

"Maybe. Maybe."

Out of those four records, there was only one Mama liked, and she damn near wore it out. "The Sign On The Highway," it was called, and after awhile I could sing it from memory.

The sign on the highway the scene of the crash . . . the people pulled over to let the hearse pass . . . their bodies were found 'neath the signboard that read . . . Beer, Wine, and Whiskey for sale just ahead. . . .

Mama couldn't help herself. She cried every time she heard it and she wanted to hear it all the time. It was a gospel song, of course, a kind of a gospel song. Mama would play it over and over, and half the time I'd come in to sit with her while she played it. We'd sit, her with a glass of tea in one hand and the other over her eyes, and me as close to her as she'd let me, both of us crying quietly so no one would notice. Uncle Jack would come in and laugh at us.

"Look at you two. You just as crazy as you can be. Look at you. Crying over some people didn't never really die. 'At's only a slide guitar and some stupid people can't make a living no other way 'cept acting the fool in front of people like you." He took some biscuits out of the towel-wrapped bowl on the table and stomped off out the screen door, while Mama went on crying and I sat still. He kicked each step as he went down.

"I swear this family's got shit for brains."

"I like your family," Shannon sometimes said, though we both knew that was a polite lie. "Your mama's a fine woman," Roseanne Pearl would agree, while she eyed my too-tight raggedy dresses. She reminded me of my stepfather's sisters looking at us out of smug, superior faces, laughing at my Mama's loose teeth and my sister's curls done up in paper scraps. Whenever the Pearls talked about my people, I'd take off and not go back for weeks. I didn't want the two parts of my life to come together.

We were living out past Henderson Road, on the other side of White Horse Highway. Up near the highway a revival tent had been erected. Some evenings I would walk up there on my own to sit outside and listen. The preacher was a shouter, something I had never liked. He'd rave and threaten, and it didn't seem as if he was ever gonna get to the invocation. I sat in the dark, trying not to think about anything, especially not about the whipping I was going to get if I stayed too long. I kept seeing my Uncle Jack in the men who stood near the highway sharing a bottle in a paper sack, black-headed men with blasted, roughhewn faces. Was it hatred or sorrow that made them look like that, their necks so stiff and their eyes so cold?

Did I look like that?

Would I look like that when I grew up? I remembered Aunt Grace putting her big hands over my ears and turning my face to catch the light, saying, "Just as well you smart; you an't never gonna be a beauty."

At least I wasn't as ugly as Shannon Pearl, I told myself, and was immediately ashamed. Shannon hadn't made herself ugly, but if I kept thinking that way I just might. Mama always said people could see your soul in your face, could see your hatefulness and lack of charity. With all the hatefulness I was trying to hide, it was a wonder I wasn't uglier than a toad in mud season.

The singing started. I sat forward on my heels and hugged my knees, humming. Revivals are funny. People get pretty enthusiastic, but they sometimes forget just which hymn it is they're singing. I grinned to myself and watched the men near the road punch each other lightly and curse in a friendly fashion.

You bastard.

You son of a bitch.

The preacher said something I didn't understand. There was a moment of silence, and then a pure tenor voice rose up into the night sky. The spit soured in my mouth. They had a real singer in there, a real gospel choir.

SWING LOW SWEET CHARIOT. . .COMING FOR TO CAR-RY ME HOME. . .AS I WALKED OUT IN THE STREETS OF LAREDO. . .SWEET JESUS. . .LIFT ME UP, LIFT ME UP IN THE AIR. . . .

The night seemed to wrap all around me like a blanket. My insides felt as if they had melted, and I could just feel the wind in my mouth. The sweet gospel music poured through me and made all my nastiness, all my jealousy and hatred, swell in my heart. I knew, I knew I was the most disgusting person in the world. I didn't deserve to live another day. I started hiccupping and crying.

"I'm sorry. Jesus, I'm sorry."

How could I live with myself? How could God stand me? Was this why Jesus wouldn't speak to my heart? The music washed over me. . .*SOFTLY AND TENDERLY.* The music was a river trying to wash me clean. I sobbed and dug my heels into the dirt, drunk on grief and that pure, pure voice. It didn't matter then if it was whiskey backstage or tongue kissing in the dressing room. Whatever it took to make that juice was necessary, was fine. I wiped my eyes and swore out loud. Get those boys another bottle, I said. Find that girl a hard-headed husband. But goddamn, get them to make that music. Make that music! Lord, make me drunk on that music.

The next Sunday I went off with Shannon and the Pearls for another gospel drive.

Driving backcountry with the Pearls meant stopping in at little country churches listening to gospel choirs. Mostly all those choirs had was a little echo of the real stuff. "Pitiful, an't it?" Shannon sounded like her father's daughter. "Organ music just can't stand against a slide guitar." I nodded, but I wasn't sure she was right.

Sometimes one pure voice would stand out, one little girl, one set of brothers whose eyes would lift when they sang. Those were the ones who could make you want to scream low against all the darkness in the world. "That one," Shannon would whisper smugly, but I didn't need her to tell me. I could always tell which one Mr. Pearl would take aside and invite over to Gaston for revival week.

"Child!" he'd say, "you got a gift from God."

Uh huh, yeah.

Sometimes I couldn't stand it. I couldn't go in one more church, hear one more choir. Never mind loving the music, why couldn't God give me a voice? I hadn't asked for thick eyelashes. I had asked for, begged for, gospel. Didn't God give a good goddamn what *I* wanted? If He'd take bastards into heaven, how come He couldn't put me in front of those hot lights and all that dispensation? Gospel singers always had money in their pockets, another bottle under their seats. Gospel singers had love and safety and the whole wide world to fall back on—women and church and red clay solid under their feet. All I wanted, I whispered, all I wanted was a piece, a piece, a little piece of it.

Shannon looked at me sympathetically.

She knows, I thought, she knows what it is to want what you are never going to have.

That July we went over to the other side of Greer, a part of the county I knew from visiting one of the cousins who worked at the airbase. Off the highway we stopped at a service station to give Mrs. Pearl a little relief from the heat.

"You ever think God maybe didn't intend us to travel on Sunday afternoon? I swear he makes it hotter than Saturday or Friday."

Mrs. Pearl sat out in the shade while Mr. Pearl went off to speak to the man that rented out the Rhythm Ranch. Shannon and I cut off across a field to check out the headstones near a stand of cotton-wood. We loved to read the mottoes and take back the good ones to Mrs. Pearl to stitch up on samplers and sell in the store. My favorites were the weird ones, like "Now He Knows" or "Too Pure." Shannon loved the ones they put up for babies, little curly headed dolls with angel wings and heartbreaking lines like "Gone To Mama, or "Gone Home."

"Silly stuff." I kicked at the pieces of clay pot that were lying every-where. Shannon turned to me, and I saw tears on her cheeks.

"No, no, it just tears me up. Think about it, losing your own little baby girl, your own little angel. Oh, I can't stand it. I just can't stand it." She gave big satisfied sobs and wiped her hands on her blue gingham pockets.

"I wish I could take me one of these home. Wouldn't you like to have one you could keep up? You could tell stories to the babies."

"You crazy."

Shannon sniffed. "You just don't understand. Mama says I've got a very tender heart."

"Uh huh." I walked away. It was too hot to fight. It was certainly too hot to cry. I kicked over some plastic flowers and a tattered green cardboard cross. This was one of the most boring trips I'd ever taken with the Pearls. I tried to remember why I'd even wanted to come. At home Mama would be making fresh iced tea, boiling up sugar water to mix in it. Reese would be slicing peaches. My stepfather would be working on the lawn mower. I swatted at mosquitoes and hoped my face wasn't sunburning. I stopped.

The music coming through the cottonwoods was gospel.

Gut-shaking, deep-bellied, powerful voices rolled through the dried leaves and hot air. Not some piddlyshit thin-voiced choir, this was the real stuff. I could feel the whiskey edge, the grief and holding on, the dark night terror and determination of real gospel.

"My God," I whispered, and it was the best My God I'd ever put out, a stretched-out, scared whisper that meant I just might start to believe He hid in cottonwoods.

There was a church there, clapboard walls standing on cement blocks and no pretense of stained-glass windows. Just yellow glass reflecting back sunlight, all the windows open to let in the breeze and let out that music.

AMAZING GRACE...HOW GREAT THOU ART...TO SAVE

*A WRETCH LIKE ME.... * A woman's voice rose and rolled over
the deeper men's voices, rolled out so strong it seemed to rustle the
leaves on the cottonwood trees.
AMEN.
LORD.
"Sweet Jesus, she can sing."
Shannon ignored me and kept pulling up wildflowers.
"You hear that? We got to tell your daddy."
Shannon turned her head to the side and stared at me with a
peculiar angry expression. "He don't handle colored. An't no money
in handling colored."
At that I froze, realizing that such a church off such a dirt road
had to be just that—a colored church. And I knew what that meant.
Of course I did. Still I heard myself whisper, "That an't one good
voice. That's a church full."
"It's colored. It's niggers." Shannon's voice was as loud as I'd ever
heard it and shrill with indignation. "My daddy don't handle niggers." She threw down her wildflowers and stomped her foot. "And
you made me say that. Mama always said a good Christian don't use
the word *nigger*. Jesus be my witness, I wouldn't have said it if you
hadn't made me."
"You crazy. You just plain crazy." My voice was shaking. The way
Shannon said *nigger* tore at me, the tone pitched exactly like the echoing sound of my stepfather's sister mouthing *trash* when she thought
I wasn't close enough to hear. Later, much later, I would even wonder what it was that she heard in my voice that made her as angry
as I was. Maybe it was the heat, maybe it was the shame we both
were feeling, or maybe it was simply that Shannon Pearl and I were
righteously tired of each other.
Shannon threw another handful of flowers at me. "I'm crazy. Me?
What do you think you are? You and your mama and your whole
family. Everybody knows you're all a bunch of drunks and thieves
and whores. Everybody knows you just come round so you can eat
off my mama's table and beg scraps of stuff we don't want no more.
Everybody knows who you are..."
I was moving before I could stop myself, my hands flying up to
slap together right in front of her face—a last minute attempt not
to hit her. "You bitch, you white-assed bitch." I wrung my hands, trying
to hold on, to keep myself from slapping her pasty, ugly face. *Don't
you never hit anybody in the face,* Mama always said.
"You little shit, you fuck-off." I put the words out as slick and

fast as any of my uncles. Shannon's mouth fell open. "You just fuck off." I kicked red dirt up onto her pink and white skirt.

Shannon's face twisted. "You an't never gonna go to another gospel show with us again! I'm gonna tell my mama what you said, what you called me, and she an't ever gonna let you come near me again."

"Your mama, your mama. You'd piss in a Pepsi bottle if your mama told you to."

"Listen to you. You. . .you trash. You nothing but trash. Your mama's trash, and your grandmama, and your whole dirty family. . ."

I hit her then. With my hand wide open, I swung at her face, but I was too angry. I was crazy angry and I tripped, falling with my hands spread onto the red dirt. My right hand slapped into a broken clay pot, hurting me so bad I could barely see Shannon's dripping flushed cheeks.

"Oh. . .shit. You. . .shit." If I could have jumped up and caught her, I would have ripped out handfuls of that cotton candy hair.

Shannon stopped moving back and watched as I pushed myself up and grabbed my right hand with my left. I was crying, I realized, the tears running down my face while behind us the choir had never stopped singing. That woman's voice still rolled over the cottonwoods. *WAS BLIND BUT NOW I SEE. . . .*

"You're ugly." I swallowed my tears and spoke very quietly. "You're God's own ugly child and you're gonna be an ugly woman. A lonely, ugly old woman."

Shannon's lips started to tremble, poking out of her face so that she was uglier than I'd ever seen her, a doll carved out of cold grease melting in the heat.

"You ugly thing," I went on. "You monster, you greasy cross-eyed stinking sweaty-faced ugly thing!" I pointed all my fingers at her and spit at her patent leather shoes. "You so ugly, your own mama don't even love you." Shannon backed off, turned around and started running.

"Mamaaaaa. . ." she wailed as she ran. I kept yelling "ugly, ugly" after her, more to keep myself from crying than to hurt her anymore. "Ugly. . .ugly. . .ugly."

Mama didn't want to know why Shannon and I had quarreled. The only thing she got angry about was Mrs. Pearl telling her that I'd hit Shannon in the face. "You can put somebody's eye out, hitting them in the face. No reason to be hitting people anyway."

"No ma'am."

"Well...." She looked at me closely. I knew she was waiting for me to tell her something, but I just kept my eyes on the table. "They should have brought you home right away, 'stead of making you sit in the car while they went all over everywhere."

"Yes ma'am." I didn't have a thing to say about Shannon Pearl.

Mama sighed tiredly, "Well, you just stay out of trouble the rest of the summer. I don't want to be explaining your behavior to other people all the time."

"No ma'am."

For most of August my stepfather was out of work, so Mama let me stay over at Aunt Alma's house. I spent my time organizing the cousins in acting out complicated stories, half of which were drawn from television programs. As long as everybody did what I told them, I was the best babysitter Aunt Alma had ever seen.

"You can be Francis Marion," I told Butch. "Reese and I will be Cherokee warriors, Patsy can be the British commander, David will be the cowardly colonist, and Dan can be a colonist on our side."

"Swamp fox, swamp fox, where have you been?" Butch began singing but Patsy cut him off. "Why do I have to be the British commander? Why can't you be the bad guy and let me be a Cherokee?"

" 'Cause you don't climb trees worth a pig's ass. Everybody knows Indians can climb trees."

"Then I get to ride the horse, and I want to ride Dan's bike, not Butch's old one."

"If she gets to ride my bike, then I want to wear your cap."

"We don't use my cap in this one. We only use my cap when we play Johnny Yuma." I was losing patience and I certainly didn't want to give up my rebel cap. Uncle Jack had brought it back from the Fort Sumter general store just before he got sent to the county farm for busting a man's jaw and breaking a window at the Cracker Blue Cafe. The cap he gave me was beautiful—grey, soft, with a slouched-forward brim, and the stars and bars stitched in yellow thread.

"Johnny Yuma," Butch started singing again, trying hard to imitate Johnny Cash's deep voice. "He roamed through the west... JOHNNY YUMA THE REBEL...He wandered alone..."

"You always wear it." Dan swatted Butch's rear end and turned back to me with a look of sweet reasonableness. "Don't matter if we're playing Frankenstein's monster, and you know didn't nobody wear no cap like that in the Frankenstein movie."

"Oh, for crying out loud." I let Dan wear my cap, but I lost interest in the swamp fox. Who'd ever heard of him before he showed up on Walt Disney?

Blue and Garvey would only play with us about half the time. They had recently taken up smoking and were busy practicing pitching pennies. When school started again, they planned to wipe out the lunch money of half the sixth grade. Meanwhile, they would only play when I proposed a plot they really liked.

"Let's play 'The Dalton Boys' again," Blue kept suggesting. He'd perfected the trick of diving off his bicycle after pretending to be shot and he loved to show it off.

"It's the Dalton *Girls*," I insisted. Reese and I had seen the movie twice and would have seen it a third time if the theater hadn't closed down.

"Well maybe, but everybody remembers the Dalton *Boys*." Blue and Garvey had seen the movie too, and hadn't gotten over how the Dalton brothers had been killed off in the first scene so the women could learn to shoot guns and rob banks. "I don't think that movie was real anyway. I bet you their sisters never robbed no banks."

"What you want to bet?" Reese challenged. She'd loved the movie as much as I had. "You think a girl can't beat your ass? You think I can't beat your ass?"

"Oh, you couldn't scare a chicken off a nest of water moccasins!"

"You're the one scared of water moccasins. Aunt Alma said you pissed your pants when she took you blackberrying, all 'count of you stepped near a little green snake. Thinking it was some old water moccasin..."

"You shut your chicken piss mouth."

"You shut yours!"

"Girls!"

"Boys!"

Aunt Alma made us break it up. She sent the boys to play in the backyard and told us girls we'd have to stay in the front.

"If you can't play together, I'll keep you apart."

"I don't want to be 'round no stupid boys anyway." Sometimes I agreed with every word out of my little sister's mouth.

"But what we gonna play now?" Patsy whined. "We can't ride the bikes in the frontyard. We can't do much of nothing in the frontyard."

I spun my rebel cap on my fist and had a sudden inspiration. "We're gonna play mean sister."

"What?" Patsy kept wiping the snot off her lip. Mama swore Patsy had had a runny nose since she was born. "She'll be wiping snot the day she's married, wiping snot the day she dies." I gave Patsy the handkerchief I'd sneaked out of my stepfather's drawer for a bandana.

"We're gonna play mean sisters," I told them all again, and I could see in my mind's eye Shannon Pearl's twisted mean face. "First we're gonna play Johnny Yuma's mean sisters, then Francis Marion's mean sisters, then Bat Masterson's. Then we'll think of somebody else."

Reese looked confused. "What do mean sisters do?"

"They do everything their brothers do. Only they do it first and fastest and meanest."

Reese still looked confused, but Patsy whooped.

"Yeah! I want to be the Rifleman's mean sister."

Patsy ran off to get Dan's old broken plastic rifle. All afternoon she pretended it was a sawed-off shotgun like the one on "Wanted: Dead or Alive." Reese finally got into it and started playing at being shot off the porch. I took Aunt Alma's butcher knife and announced that I was gonna be Jim Bowie's mean sister, and no one was to bother me.

I practiced sticking Aunt Alma's knife into the porch and listened to the boys cursing in the backyard. I was mean, I decided. I was mean and vicious, and all I really wanted to be doing was sticking that knife in Roseanne Pearl's fancy sewing. She'd called me an evil child when Shannon told her what I'd said. She hadn't wanted to hear what her darling daughter had said to me.

That evening, Patsy entertained the whole family by running up and down the porch steps yelling, "Ten-four, Ten-four" until she knocked over Aunt Grace's glass of tea.

"What in God's name are you playing at, child?"

"I was being Broderick Crawford's mean sister," Patsy wailed, wiping her nose.

"His what?" Uncle Bo started laughing into his glass. "His what!" He rocked back on his cane-bottom chair and ground his cigarette out on the porch floor. Aunt Alma shook her head and looked at Patsy like she had gone crazy.

"Broderick Crawford's mean sister! My Lord, what they don't think up."

Patsy was humiliated and angry. She pointed at me. "She told me about it. She told me I could."

Bo reached out and slapped my fanny. "Girl, you got a mind that scares me." He swatted me again, but lightly, and he kept grinning.

"Broderick Crawford's mean sister."

I didn't care. I played mean sister all summer long.

One Sunday late in August, Shannon Pearl called our house. "I'm not gonna apologize," she said right away, as if no time at all had passed. Her voice sounded strange after not hearing it for so long.

"I don't care what you do," I told her. I held the phone with my shoulder and picked my cuticles with my fingernails.

"Stop that," Mama said, as she went by me on her way to the kitchen.

"Yes ma'am," I said automatically.

"What's that?" Shannon sounded hopeful.

"I was talking to my mama. Why'd you call me?"

There was a sigh, and then Shannon's voice cleared a couple of times. "Well, I thought I should. No sense us fighting over something so silly, anyway. I bet you can't even remember what it was about."

"I remember," I told her, though I really couldn't have said what had started us fighting and my voice sounded cold even to me. For a moment I was ashamed, then angry. Why should I care if I hurt her feelings? Who was she to me?

"My mama said I could call you," Shannon whispered. "She said I could ask you over this Sunday. We're gonna have a barbecue for some of Daddy's people from Mississippi. They're bringing us some Georgia peaches and some egg-shell pecans." I bit at my thumbnail and said nothing.

"You could ask your mama if you could come," Shannon's voice sounded breathless and desperate, almost squeaky. "If you wanted to," she added. I wondered what she had told her mama in order to get her to agree I could come over. Out on the porch Reese had started shouting at Patsy.

"You don't even know how to play this game!"

Why should I go to the Pearls' house and watch her fat relatives eat themselves sick?

"Mama gave me a record player," Shannon said suddenly. "I got a bunch of records for it."

"Yeah?"

"Lots of 'em." I heard her mother saying something in the background. "I got to go. Are you gonna come?"

"Maybe. I don't know. I'll think about it." I hung up the phone and saw Mama was watching me from the kitchen. "Shannon wants me to come over to her house this Sunday. They're having a barbecue."

"You want to go?"

"Maybe. I don't know." Mama nodded and handed me a towel. "Well, you tell me before Sunday. I an't gonna want no surprises on Sunday morning. I might want to spend the whole day in bed, you never can tell." Mama laughed, and I ran over and hugged her. I loved it when she laughed like that. It made the whole house feel warm and safe.

"I might want to go on a trip myself." Mama laughed again and slapped my behind lightly. "But I an't going nowhere till we get these dishes done girl, and it's your turn to dry."

"Yes ma'am."

I didn't plan to go. I really didn't. I certainly didn't call Shannon back and I didn't say anything to Mama either. But Sunday afternoon I started walking toward Shannon's house, carrying Reese's tin bucket as if I was gonna go hunting for muscadines. Along the way I shook the vines and tried to imagine swinging from them. Every time Reese or I tried, we wound up falling on our behinds. Maybe they had a different kind in Africa. Probably didn't grow muscadines either.

I hummed as I walked, snatches of Mama's favorite hymns and mine, alternating between "Somebody Touched Me" and "Oh Sinner Man." Reese always sang it as "Whoa Sinner Man," which invariably made Uncle Jack bark out his donkey's bray laugh. Actually it looked like we weren't going to see Uncle Jack until next summer. He'd got into another fight down at the county farm, and Aunt Grace said a bunch of men had held him down and shaved all his black hair off. I tried to imagine him bald-headed.

"That'll slow down his womanizing." Aunt Grace had been almost pleased.

"What's *womanizing?*" Reese hadn't learned yet that asking questions about most things the aunts said to each other just got you pushed outside. I'd tried to tell her that if she ever wanted to learn anything, she should just shut up and listen and try to figure it out later.

"What are you doing listening to other people's business?" Mama had been really angry. "You get out of here, all of you."

"See what you did." I'd been righteously indignant. I wasn't used to being put out with the little kids. "Now we'll never know why they shaved his head."

"Oh, I know that already." Reese gave me a smirk and put her arm around Patsy. "Granny said he tried to cut some fellow's dick off."

I'd never come up to the Pearl's house from the back before. I usually came down the road from the Sears Tire Center, but that Sunday I cut through the backyards of the big houses on Tyson Circle and through the parking lot of the Roberts Dairy Drive-In. Mrs. Pearl had planted magnolia and mums all along the back of their property so no one could see that parking lot, and I had to wiggle past some of the mums that were planted close up to their fence.

There were a lot of people there, and they all looked like Pearls. Big puffy men stood around holding massive glasses of iced tea and grinning at skinny pale women with thin flyaway hair. Some kids were running around over near the driveway where some big boys were taking turns cranking an ice-cream maker. Two card tables had been set up in addition to the big redwood picnic table Mrs. Pearl was so proud of getting last year. It looked like people had already been eating but the charcoal grill was still smoldering, and Shannon Pearl was standing beside it looking as miserable as any human being could.

I stood still and watched her. She was playing with a long-handled fork and looking over every now and then at the other children playing. Her face was flushed pink and sweaty, and she looked swollen in her orange and white organdy dress. I remembered how Mama said Mrs. Pearl just didn't know how to dress her daughter.

"She shouldn't put her in all that embroidery as fat as that child is, it just makes her look bigger."

I agreed. Shannon looked like a sausage stuffed in a too-small casing. She also looked like she had been crying. Past the tables, Mrs. Pearl was sitting with half a dozen wispy, thin women, two of whom were holding babies.

"Precious. Precious," I heard someone exclaim in a reedy voice.

"You fat old thing." One of Shannon's cousins ran past her and play-whispered loud in her ear. "You must'a eat nothing but pork since you was born. Turned you into the hog you are." He laughed and ran on. Shannon pulled off her glasses and started cleaning them on her skirt.

"Jesus shit," I whispered to myself.

I had always suspected that I was the only friend Shannon Pearl had in the world. That was part of what made me feel so mean and evil around her, knowing that I didn't really care enough about her to be her friend. But hearing her cousin talk to her that way brought back to me the first time I'd met her, the way I'd loved her stubborn pride, the righteous rage she turned on her tormentors. She didn't look righteous at that moment. She looked tired and hurt and a-shamed. Her face made me feel sick and angry, and guilty about her all over again.

I kicked at the short wooden fence for a moment and then swung one leg up to climb over. All right, she was a little monster, but she was my friend and the kind of monster I could understand. Twenty feet away from me, Shannon sniffed and reached for the can of light-er fluid by the grill. She hadn't even seen me watching her.

Afterward, people kept asking me what happened.

"Where were you?" Mr. Carson, the County Sheriff, kept asking me, "and what exactly did you see?" He never gave me a chance to tell him. Maybe because it was hard to hear over Mrs. Pearl scream-ing. With all the confusion and shouting, his questions sounded both formal and meaningless.

"Uh huh, and where were you?" He kept looking over his shoul-der toward the grill and the sputtering fat fire.

I knew then he hadn't heard a word I said. But Mrs. Pearl did. She heard me clear, and I thought she was gonna come right over the people holding her. She was trying to get her hands on me. She kept screaming "YOU!" like I had done something myself, but all I had done was watch. I was sure of that. I had never gotten two steps past the fence.

Shannon had put her glasses back on. She had the lighter fluid can in one hand, and she took up that long-handled fork in the oth-er. She poked the coals with the fork and sprayed them with the flu-id from the can. The can made a popping noise as she squeezed it. She was trying to get more of the coals burning, it seemed. Or may-be she just liked the way the flames leaped up. She sprayed and sprayed, and pulled back and sprayed again.

Shannon shook her hand. I heard the lighter fluid can sputter and suck air, and then I saw the flame run up right to the can. It looked like the flame went out. Then it came back with a boom. The can exploded, and fire ballooned out in a great rolling ball.

Shannon didn't even scream. She had her mouth wide open, and it seemed as if she just breathed the flames in. Her glasses went opaque, her eyes disappeared, and all around her skull her fine hair stood up in a crown of burning glory. Her dress whooshed and disappeared in orange-yellow smoky flames. I saw the fork fall, the wooden han-

dle burning. I saw Mrs. Pearl come to her feet and start to run toward her daughter. I saw all the men dropping their iced tea glasses.
I saw Shannon stagger and stumble from side to side, and then fall
in a heap. Her dress was gone. I saw the smoke turn black and oily.
I saw Shannon Pearl disappear from this world.

They held the funeral at Bushy Creek Baptist. Mrs. Pearl insisted on laying an intricately embroidered baby blanket over the coffin.
I gave it one glance and then kept my head down. Mrs. Pearl had
put a baby cherub with pink cheeks and yellow hair on the spot that
was probably covering Shannon's blackened features. I kept my hand
in Mama's and my mouth shut tight.

"Did you ever see her?" Mrs. Pearl was saying to the preacher
they'd brought in from their family church in Mississippi. "She was
just an angel of the Lord."

The preacher nodded and laid his hands on top of Mrs. Pearl's
where she was hugging close a great bunch of yellow mums. Beyond
them, the choir director had one hand on Mr. Pearl's elbow. Mr. Pearl
was as grey as a dead man. I watched from under my lowered lashes
while the choir director pushed a paper cup into Mr. Pearl's hand
and whispered in his ear. Mr. Pearl nodded and sipped steadily. He
kept looking over at his wife and the flowers she was gripping so tightly.

"She loved babies, you know. She was always a friend to the less
fortunate...all her little friends are here today...and she could sing.
Oh! You should have heard her sing."

I remembered Shannon's hoarse wavering voice humming in the
backseat of her daddy's car after she had told me a particularly horrible story. Was it possible Mrs. Pearl had never heard her daughter
sing? I looked over to Mr. Pearl and saw his head go down again.
If it had been me in that ball of flame, would they have come to my
funeral?

Mrs. Pearl lifted her face from the closely held flowers. Her watery eyes flickered back and forth across the pews. She doesn't understand anything, I thought. Mrs. Pearl's eyes moved over me
sightlessly while her hands gripped and crushed the flowers pressed
against her neck. She started to moan suddenly like a bird caught
in a blackberry bush, moaning softly, tonelessly, while the preacher
carefully pushed her down into the front pew. The choir director's
wife ran over and put her arm around Mrs. Pearl while the preacher
desperately signaled the choir to start a hymn. Their voices rose
smoothly while Mrs. Pearl's moan went on and on, rising into the

close sweaty air, a song with no meter, no rhythm—but gospel, the purest gospel, a song of absolute hopeless grief.

I turned and pushed my face into my mama's dress. Nothing could cover the persistent smell of barbecue.

I'M WORKING ON MY CHARM

I'm working on my charm.

It was one of those parties where everyone pretends to know everyone else. My borrowed silk blouse kept pulling out of my skirt, so I tried to stay with my back to the buffet and ignore the bartender who had a clear view of my problem. The woman who brushed my arm was a friend of the director of the organization where I worked, a woman who was known for her wardrobe and sudden acts of well-publicized generosity. She tossed her hair back when she saw me and laughed like an old familiar friend. "Southerners are so charming, I always say, giving their children such clever names."

She had a wine glass in one hand and a cherry tomato in the other, and she gestured with that tomato—a wide, witty, "charmed" gesture I do not remember ever seeing in the South. "I just love yours. There was a girl at school had a name like yours, two names said as one actually. Barbara-Jean, I think, or Ruth-Anne. I can't remember anymore, but she was the sweetest, most soft-spoken girl. I just loved her."

She smiled again, her eyes looking over my head at someone else. She leaned in close to me, "It's so wonderful that you can be with us, you know. Some of the people who have worked here, well. . .you know, well, we have so much to learn from you—gentility, you know, courtesy, manners, charm, all of that."

For a moment I was dizzy, overcome with the curious sensation of floating out of the top of my head. It was as if I looked down on all the other people in that crowded room, all of them sipping their wine and half of them eating cherry tomatoes. I watched the woman beside me click her teeth against the beveled edge of her wine glass and heard the sound of my mother's voice hissing in my left ear, *Yankeeeeeees!* It was all I could do not to nod.

When I was sixteen I worked counter with my mama back of a Moses Drugstore planted in the middle of a Highway 50 shopping mall. I was trying to save money to go to college, and ritually, every night, I'd pour my tips into a can on the back of my dresser. Sometimes my mama'd throw in a share of hers to encourage me, but mostly hers was spent even before we got home—at the Winn Dixie at the far end of the mall or the Maryland Fried Chicken right next to it.

Mama taught me the real skills of being a waitress—how to get an order right, get the drinks there first and the food as fast as possible so it would still be hot, and to do it all with an expression of relaxed good humor. "You don't have to smile," she explained, "but it does help." "Of course," she had to add, "don't go 'round like a grinning fool. Just smile like you know what you're doing, and never *look* like you're in a hurry." I found it difficult to keep from looking like I was in a hurry, especially when I got out of breath running from steam table to counter. Worse, moving at the speed I did, I tended to sway a little and occasionally lost control of a plate.

"Never," my mama told me, "serve food someone has seen fall to the floor. It's not only bad manners, it'll get us all in trouble. Take it in the back, clean it off, and return it to the steam table." After awhile I decided I could just run to the back, count to ten, and take it back out to the customer with an apology. Since I usually just dropped biscuits, cornbread, and baked potatoes—the kind of stuff that would roll on a plate—I figured brushing it off was sufficient. But once, in a real rush to an impatient customer, I watched a ten-ounce T-bone slip right off the plate, flip in the air, and smack the rubber floor mat. The customer's mouth flew open, and I saw my mama's eyes shoot fire. Hurriedly I picked it up by the bone and ran to the back with it. I was running water on it when Mama came in the back room.

"All right," she snapped, "you are not to run, you are not even to walk fast. And," she added, taking the meat out of my fingers and dropping it into the open waste can, "you are not, not ever to drop anything as expensive as that again." I watched smoky frost from the leaky cooler float up toward her blonde curls, and I promised her tearfully that I wouldn't.

The greater skills Mama taught me were less tangible than rules about speed and smiling. What I needed most from her had a lot to do with being as young as I was, as naive, and quick to believe the stories put across the counter by all those travelers heading North. Mama always said I was the smartest of her daughters and the most foolish. I believed everything I read in books, and most of the stuff I heard on the TV, and all of Mama's carefully framed warnings never seemed to quite slow down my capacity to take people as who they wanted me to think they were. I tried hard to be like my mama but, as she kept complaining, I was just too quick to trust—badly in need of a little practical experience.

My practical education began the day I started work. The first comment by the manager was cryptic but to the point. "Well, sixteen." Harriet smiled, looking me up and down, "At least you'll up the ante." Mama's friend, Mabel, came over and squeezed my arm. "Don't get nervous, young one. We'll keep moving you around. You'll never be left alone."

Mabel's voice was reassuring even if her words weren't, and I worked her station first. A family of four children, parents, and a grandmother took her biggest table. She took their order with a wide smile, but as she passed me going down to the ice drawer, her teeth were point on point. "Fifty cents," she snapped, and went on. Helping her clean the table thirty-five minutes later I watched her pick up two lone quarters and repeat "fifty cents," this time in a mournfully conclusive tone.

It was a game all the waitresses played. There was a butter bowl on the back counter where the difference was kept, the difference between what you guessed and what you got. No one had to play, but most of the women did. The rules were simple. You had to make your guess at the tip *before* the order was taken. Some of the women would cheat a little, bringing the menus with the water glasses and saying, "I want ya'll to just look this over carefully. We're serving one fine lunch today." Two lines of conversation and most of them could walk away with a guess within five cents.

However much the guess was off went into the bowl. If you said fifty cents and got seventy-five cents, then twenty-five cents went to the bowl. Even if you said seventy-five cents and got fifty cents instead, you had to throw in that quarter—guessing high was as bad as guessing short. "We used to just count the short guesses," Mabel explained, "but this makes it more interesting."

Once Mabel was sure she'd get a dollar and got stiffed instead. She was so mad she counted out that dollar in nickels and pennies, and poured it into the bowl from a foot in the air. It made a very satisfying angry noise, and when those people came back a few weeks

later no one wanted to serve them. Mama stood back by the phar-
macy sign smoking her Pall Mall cigarette and whispered in my direction, "Yankees." I was sure I knew just what she meant.

At the end of each week, the women playing split the butter bowl
evenly.

Mama said I wasn't that good a waitress, but I made up for it
in eagerness. Mabel said I made up for it in "tail." "Those salesmen
sure do like how you run back to that steam table," she said with
a laugh, but she didn't say it where Mama could hear. Mama said
it was how I smiled.

"You got a heartbreaker's smile," she told me. "You make them
think of when they were young." Behind her back, Mabel gave me
her own smile, and a long slow shake of her head.

Whatever it was, by the end of the first week I'd earned four dollars more in tips than my mama. It was almost embarrassing. But then
they turned over the butter bowl and divided it evenly between everyone but me. I stared and Mama explained. "Another week and you
can start adding to the pot. Then you'll get a share. For now just
write down two dollars on Mr. Aubrey's form."

"But I made a lot more than that," I told her.

"Honey, the tax people don't need to know that." Her voice was
patient. "Then when you're in the pot, just report your share. That
way we all report the same amount. They expect that."

"Yeah, they don't know nothing about initiative," Mabel added,
rolling her hips in illustration of her point. It made her heavy bosom
move dramatically, and I remembered times I'd seen her do that at
the counter. It made me feel even more embarrassed and angry.

When we were alone I asked Mama if she didn't think Mr. Aubrey
knew that everyone's reports on their tips were faked.

"He doesn't say what he knows," she replied, "and I don't imagine he's got a reason to care."

I dropped the subject and started the next week guessing on my
tips.

Salesmen and truckers were always a high guess. Women who
came with a group were low, while women alone were usually a fair
twenty-five cents on a light lunch—if you were polite and brought
them their coffee first. It was 1966, after all, and a hamburger cost
sixty-five cents. Tourists were more difficult. I learned that noisy kids
meant a small tip, which seemed the highest injustice. Maybe it was
a kind of defensive arrogance that made the parents of those kids

leave so little, as if they were saying, "Just because little Kevin gave you a headache and poured ketchup on the floor doesn't mean I owe you anything."

Early morning tourists who asked first for tomato juice, lemon, and coffee were a bonus. They were almost surely leaving the Jamaica Inn just up the road, which had a terrible restaurant but served the strongest drinks in the county. If you talked softly you never got less than a dollar, and sometimes for nothing more than juice, coffee, and aspirin.

I picked it up. In three weeks I started to really catch on and started making sucker bets like the old man who ordered egg salad. Before I even carried the water glass over, I snapped out my counter rag, turned all the way around, and said, "five." Then as I turned to the stove and the rack of menus, I mouthed, "dollars."

Mama frowned while Mabel rolled her shoulders and said, "An't we growing up fast!"

I just smiled my heartbreaker's smile and got the man his sandwich. When he left I snapped that five dollar bill loudly five times before I put it in my apron pocket. "My mama didn't raise no fool," I told the other women, who laughed and slapped my behind like they were glad to see me cutting up.

But Mama took me with her on her break. We walked up toward the Winn Dixie where she could get her cigarettes cheaper than in the drugstore.

"How'd you know?" she asked.

" 'Cause that's what he always leaves," I told her.

"What do you mean *always?*"

"Every Thursday evening when I close up." I said it knowing she was going to be angry.

"He leaves you a five dollar bill every Thursday night!" Her voice sounded strange, not angry exactly but not at all pleased either.

"Always," I said, and I added, "and he pretty much always has egg salad."

Mama stopped to light her last cigarette. Then she just stood there for a moment, breathing deeply around the Pall Mall and watching me while my face got redder and redder.

"You think you can get along without it?" she asked finally.

"Why?" I asked her. "I don't think he's going to stop."

"Because," she said, dropping the cigarette and walking on, "you're not working any more Thursday nights."

On Sundays the counter didn't open until after church at one o'clock. But at one sharp, we started serving those big gravy lunches and went right on till four. People would come in prepared to sit and eat big—coffee, salad, country fried steak with potatoes and gravy, or ham with red-eye gravy and carrots and peas. You'd also get a side of hog's head biscuits and a choice of three pies for dessert.

Tips were as choice as the pies, but Sunday had its trials. Too often, some tight-browed couple would come in at two o'clock and order breakfast—fried eggs and hash browns. When you told them we didn't serve breakfast on Sundays, they'd get angry.

"Look girl," they might say, "just bring me some of that ham you're serving those people, only bring me eggs with it. You can do that," and the contempt in their voices clearly added, "even you."

It would make me mad as sin. "Sir, we don't cook on the grill on Sundays. We only have what's on the Sunday menu. When you make up your mind, let me know."

"Tourists," I'd mutter to Mama.

"No, Yankees," she'd say, and Mabel would nod.

Then she might go over with an offer of boiled eggs, that ham, and a biscuit. She'd talk nice, drawling like she never did with me or friends, while she moved slower than you'd think a wide-awake person could. "Uh huh," she'd say, and "shore-nuf," and offer them honey for their biscuits or tell them how red-eye gravy is made, or talk about how sorry it is that we don't serve grits on Sunday. That couple would grin wide and start slowing their words down, while the regulars would choke on their coffee. Mama never bet on the tip, just put it all into the pot, and it was usually enough to provoke a round of applause after the couple was safely out the door.

Mama said nothing about it except the first time when she told me, "Yankees eat boiled eggs for breakfast," which may not sound like much, but had the force of a powerful insult. It was a fact that the only people we knew who ate boiled eggs in the morning were those stray tourists and people on the TV set who we therefore assumed had to be Yankees.

Yankees ate boiled eggs, laughed at grits but ate them in big helpings, and had plenty of money to leave outrageous tips but might leave nothing for no reason that I could figure out. It wasn't the accent that marked Yankees. They talked different, but all kinds of different. There seemed to be a great many varieties of them, not just

Northerners, but Westerners, Canadians, Black people who talked oddly enough to show they were foreign, and occasionally strangers who didn't even speak English. Some were friendly, some deliberately nasty. All of them were Yankees, strangers, unpredictable people with an enraging attitude of superiority who would say the rudest things as if they didn't know what an insult was.

"They're the ones the world was made for," Harriet told me late one night. "You and me, your mama, all of us, we just hold a place in the landscape for them. Far as they're concerned, once we're out of sight we just disappear."

Mabel plain hated them. Yankees didn't even look when she rolled her soft wide hips. "Son of a bitch," she'd say when some fish-eyed, clipped-tongue stranger would look right through her and leave her less than fifteen cents. "He must think we get fat on the honey of his smile." Which was even funnier when you'd seen that the man hadn't smiled at all.

"But give me an inch of edge and I can handle them," she'd tell me. "Sweets, you just stretch that drawl. Talk like you're from Mississippi, and they'll eat it up. For some reason, Yankees got strange sentimental notions about Mississippi."

"They're strange about other things too," Mama would throw in. "They think they can ask you personal questions just 'cause you served them a cup of coffee." Some salesman once asked her where she got her hose with the black thread sewed up the back and Mama hadn't forgiven him yet.

But the thing everyone told me and told me again was that you just couldn't trust yourself with them. Nobody bet on Yankee tips, they might leave anything. Once someone even left a New York City subway token. Mama thought it a curiosity but not the equivalent of real money. Another one ordered one cup of coffee to go and twenty packs of sugar.

"They made 'road-liquor' out of it," Mabel said. "Just add an ounce of vodka and set it down by the engine exhaust for a month or so. It'll cook up into a bitter poison that'll knock you cross-eyed."

It sounded dangerous to me, but Mabel didn't think so. "Not that I would drink it," she'd say, "but I wouldn't fault a man who did."

They stole napkins, not one or two but a boxful at a time. Before we switched to sugar packets, they'd come in, unfold two or three napkins, open them like diapers, and fill them up with sugar before they left. Then they might take the knife and spoon to go with it. Once I watched a man take out a stack of napkins I was sure he was going to walk off with. But instead he sat there for thirty minutes making notes on them, then balled them all up and threw them away when he left.

My mama was scandalized by that. "And right over there on the shelf is a notebook selling for ten cents. What's wrong with these people?"

"They're living in the movies," Mabel whispered, looking back toward the counter.

"Yeah, Bette Davis movies," I added.

"I don't know about the movies." Harriet put her hand on Mama's shoulder. "But they don't live in the real world with the rest of us."

"No," Mama said, "they don't."

I take a bite of cherry tomato and hear Mama's voice again. *No,* she says.

"No," I say. I tuck my blouse into my skirt and shift in my shoes. If I close my eyes, I can see Mabel's brightly rouged cheekbones, Harriet's pitted skin, and my mama's shadowed brown eyes. When I go home tonight I'll write her about this party and imagine how she'll laugh about it all. The woman who was talking to me has gone off across the room to the other bar. People are giving up nibbling and going on to more serious eating. One of the men I work with every day comes over with a full plate and a wide grin.

"Boy," he drawls around a bite of the cornbread I contributed to the buffet, "I bet you sure can cook."

"Bet on it," I say, with my Mississippi accent. I swallow the rest of a cherry tomato and give him my heartbreaker's smile.

STEAL AWAY

My hands shake when I am hungry, and I have always been hungry. Not for food; I have always had enough biscuit-fat to last me. In college I got breakfast, lunch, and dinner with my dormitory fees, but my restless hunger didn't abate. It was having only four dollars till the end of the month and not enough coming in then. I sat at a lunch table with the girls who planned to go to the movies for the afternoon, counting three dollars in worn bills, the rest in coins, over and over in my pocket. I couldn't go see any movies.

I went, instead, downtown to steal. I became what had always been expected of me—a thief. Dangerous, but careful. Wanting everything, I tamed my anger, smiling wide and innocent. With the help of that smile I stole toilet paper from the Burger King restroom, magazines from the lower shelves at 7-11, and sardines from the deli—sliding those little cans down my jeans to where I had drawn the cuffs tight with rubber bands. I lined my pockets with plastic bags for a trip to the local Winn Dixie, where I could collect smoked oysters from the gourmet section and fresh grapes from the open bins of produce. From the hobby shop in the same shopping center, I pocketed metal snaps to replace the rubber bands on my pant leg cuffs and metal guitar picks I could use to pry loose and switch price tags on items too big to carry away. Anything small enough to fit a palm walked out with me, anything round to fit an armpit, anything thin enough to carry between my belly and belt. The smallest, sharpest, most expensive items rested behind my teeth, behind that smile that remained my ultimate shield.

On the day that I was turned away from registration because my scholarship check was late, I dressed myself in my Sunday best and went downtown to the Hilton Hotel. There was a Methodist Outreach Convention with meetings in all the ballrooms, and a hospitality suite. I walked from room to room filling a JCPenney's shopping bag with cut class ashtrays showing the Hilton logo and faceted wine glasses marked only with the dregs of grape juice. I dragged the bag out to St. Pete beach and sailed those ashtrays off the pier like frisbees. Then I waited for sunset to toss the wine glasses high enough to see the red and purple reflections as they flipped end over end. Each piece shattered ecstatically on the tar black rocks under the pier, throwing up glass fragments into the spray. Sight and sound, it was better than a movie.

The president of the college invited all of the scholarship students over for tea or wine. He served cheese that had to be cut from a great block with delicate little knives. I sipped wine, toothed cheese, talked politely, and used my smile. The president's wife nodded at me and put her pink fleshy hand on my shoulder. I put my own hand on hers and gave one short squeeze. She started but didn't back away, and I found myself giggling at her attempts to tell us all a funny story. She flushed and told us how happy she was to have us in her home. I smiled and told her how happy I was to have come, my jacket draped loosely over the wine glasses I had hooked in my belt. Walking back to the dorm, I slipped one hand into my pocket, carefully fingering two delicate little knives.

Junior year my scholarship was cut yet again, and I became nervous that working in the mailroom wouldn't pay for all I needed. St. Vincent De Paul offered me a ransom, paying a dime apiece for plates and trays carted off from the cafeteria. Glasses were only good for three cents and hard to carry down on the bus without breaking, but sheets from the alumni guest room provided the necessary padding. My roommate complained that I made her nervous, always carrying boxes in and out. She moved out shortly after Christmas, and I chewed my nails trying to come up with a way to carry her mattress down to St. Vincent De Paul. I finally decided it was hopeless, and spent the rest of the holidays reading Jean Genet and walking through the art department hallways.

They had hardwood stools in the studios, and stacking fileboxes no one had opened in years. I wore a cloth cap when I took them, and my no-nonsense expression. I was so calm that one of the professors helped me clear paper off the third one. He was distracted, discussing Jackson Pollack with a very pale woman whose hands were marked with artist's tush. "Glad they finally decided to get these out of here," was all he said to me, never once looking up into my face.

My anger came up from my stomach with an acid taste. I went back for his clipboard and papers, but his desk was locked and my file broke on the rim. In compensation I took the silk lining out of the pockets of the corduroy coat he'd left thrown over a stool. The silk made a lemongrass sachet I gave my mother for her birthday, and every time I saw him in that jacket I smiled.

My sociology professor had red hair, forty shelves of books, four children, and an entirely cordial relationship with her ex-husband. When she invited me to dinner, I did not understand what she wanted with me. I watched her closely and kept my hands in my pockets. She talked about her divorce and the politics in the department, how she had worked for John F. Kennedy in 1960 and demonstrated for civil rights in Little Rock in '65. There were lots of books she could lend me, she insisted, but didn't say exactly which ones. She poured me Harvey's Bristol Cream, trailing her fingers across my wrist when I took the glass. Then she shook her head nervously and tried to persuade me to talk about myself, interrupting only to get me to switch topics as she moved restlessly from her rocking chair to a bolster to the couch beside me. She did not want to hear about my summers working in the mop factory, but she loved my lies about hitchhiking cross-country.

"Meet me for lunch on Monday," she insisted, while her eyes behind her glasses kept glancing at me, turning away and turning back. My palms were sweaty, but I nodded yes. At the door she stopped me, and put her hand out to touch my face.

"Your family is very poor, aren't they?"

My face froze and burned at the same time. "Not really," I told her, "not anymore." She nodded and smiled, and the heat in my face went down my body in waves.

I didn't want to go on Monday but made myself. Her secretary was confused when I asked about lunch. "I don't have anything written down about it," she said, without looking up from her calendar.

After class that afternoon the sociology professor explained her absence with a story about one of her children who had been bitten by a dog, "but not seriously. Come on Thursday," she insisted, but on Thursday neither she nor her secretary was there. I stood in the doorway to her office and tilted my head back to take in her shelves of books. I wanted to pocket them all, but at the same time I didn't want anything of hers. Trembling, I reached and pulled out the fattest book on the closest shelf. It was a hardbound edition of *Sadism in the Movies*, with a third of the pages underlined in red. It fit easily in my backpack, and I stopped in the Student Union bookstore on the way back to the dorm to buy a Hershey's bar and steal a bright blue pen.

On the next Monday, she apologized again, and again invited me to go to lunch the next day. I skipped lunch but slipped in that afternoon to return her book, now full of my bright blue comments. In its spot on the shelf there was now a collection of the essays of Georges Bataille, still unmarked. By the time I returned it on Friday, heavy blue ink stains showed on the binding itself.

Eventually we did have lunch. She talked to me about how hard it was to be a woman alone in a college town, about how all the male professors treated her like a fool, and yet how hard she worked. I nodded.

"You read so much," I whispered.

"I keep up," she agreed with me.

"So do I," I smiled.

She looked nervous and changed the subject but let me walk her back to her office. On her desk, there was a new edition of Malinowski's *The Sexual Life of Savages*. I laid my notebook down on top of it, and took them both when I left. Malinowski was a fast read. I had that one back a day later. She was going through her datebook looking for a free evening we could have dinner. But exams were coming up so soon. I smiled and nodded and backed out the door. The secretary, used to seeing me come and go, didn't even look up.

I took no other meals with professors; didn't trust myself in their houses. But I studied their words, gestures, jokes, and quarrels to see just how they were different from me. I limited my outrage to their office shelves, working my way through their books one at a time, carefully underlining my favorite passages in dark blue ink—occasionally covering over their own faded marks. I continued to take the sociology professor's classes but refused to stay after to talk, and when she called my name in the halls, I would just smile and keep walking. Once she sat beside me in a seminar and put her hand on the back of my neck where I was leaning back in my chair. I turned and saw she was biting her lips. I remembered her saying, "Your family is very poor, aren't they?" I kept my face expressionless and looked forward again. That was the afternoon I made myself a pair of harem pants out of the gauze curtains from the infirmary.

My parents came for graduation, Mama taking the day off from the diner, my stepfather walking slow in his backbrace. They both were bored at the lunch, uncomfortable and impatient to have the ceremony be over so we could pack my boxes in the car and leave. Mama kept pulling at the collar of my robe while waiting for the call for me to join my class. She was so nervous she kept rocking back on her heels and poked my statistics professor with her elbow as he tried to pass.

"Quite something, your daughter," he grinned, as he shook my mama's hand. Mama and I could both tell he was uncomfortable, so she just nodded, not knowing what to say. "We're expecting great things of her," he added, and quickly joined the other professors on the platform, their eyes roaming over the parents headed for the elevated rows at the sides and back of the hall. I saw my sociology professor sharing a quick sip from the Dean's pocket flask. She caught me watching, and her face flushed a dull reddish grey. I smiled as widely as ever I had, and held that smile through the long slow ceremony that followed, the walk up to get my diploma, and the confused milling around that followed the moment when we were all supposed to throw our tassels over to the other side. Some of the students threw their mortarboards drunkenly into the air, but I tucked mine under my arm and found my parents before they had finished shaking the cramps out of their legs.

"Sure went on forever," Mama whispered, as we walked toward the exit.

The statistics professor was standing near the door telling a tall Black woman, "Quite something, your son. We're expecting great things of him."

I laughed and tucked my diploma in Mama's bag for the walk back to the dormitory. People were packing station wagons, U-Haul trailers, and bulging little sedans. Our Pontiac was almost full and my face was starting to ache from smiling, but I made a quick trip down into the dormitory basement anyway. There was a vacuum cleaner and two wooden picture frames I'd stashed behind the laundry room doors that I knew would fit perfectly in the Pontiac's trunk. Mama watched me carry them up but said nothing. Daddy only laughed and revved the engine while we swung past the auditorium. At the entrance to the campus I got them to pull over and look back at the scattered buildings. It was a rare moment, and for a change my hunger wasn't bothering me at all. But while my parents waited, I climbed out and pulled the commemorative roses off the welcome sign. I got back in the car and piled them into my mama's lap.

"Quite something, my daughter," she laughed, and hugged the flowers to her breast. She rocked in her seat as my stepfather gunned the engine and spun the tires pulling out. I grinned while she laughed.

"Quite something."

It was the best moment I'd had in four years.

MONKEYBITES

In college I contemplated a career in biology for one long year, and rats—fat grey ones with miniscule wires in their skulls or slender white ones trailing colored threads to mark the buried electrodes. The animal labs were in a cinder-block building set away from the campus. I went there like a pilgrim to stare into the cages and finger the plush on a monkey's neck, the monkey bent to a frame that kept his razor teeth from my flesh. After a while the teeth were gone with the larynx, and he only spat when I came to see him.

It hurt me that he could not bite; the rats at least kept their teeth. I told myself that the security of a career in science demanded sacrifice. I would have to get used to rats with wires and monkeys without teeth. But it was hard, hard. I hated the white-washed walls and the raw, shrinking creatures under my hands as much as the implacable mechanical motions of the professors in rubber gloves. After I got the job of cleaning up the lab, my dreams were full of monkeys' teeth and the sybilant scratches of rats' nails on formica counters. On those rare nights when Toni and I could sleep over at a friend's house in the city, I would wake shuddering, feeling her arms around me like the wires that trussed the monkeys.

"You are one restless woman," Toni would tell me in the morning, showing me the scratches I'd made on her arms and back. "Can't lie still to save your life." More out of guilt than desire, I'd kiss her shoulders and slide down between her legs to ease with my tongue what I could not cure with words. I felt about oral sex with Toni the way my roommate in the dorm felt about transcendental meditation. At the point at which my neck began to ache and my fingers spasmed on her thighs, I would begin to feel righteous. The longer it took to get her off, and the greater the ache in my neck and back, the farther away I would go in my mind until finally it was as if I were not making love to Toni, but to myself. I became a point of concentration, icy and hot at the same time. When she began to babble those love words that meant she was just about to come, my own thighs would shake sympathetically. I rarely came making love to Toni, but nothing made me feel so balanced as an hour or two pushing my tongue between her swollen labia. It was expiation and penance. It was redemption.

But for Toni, sex was a matter of commitment; making love was a bond itself. She had her own cage, her own need for expiation, and she hated the way I could go away into my own head, the distance between us that she could not cross. She wanted a bridge across my nerves, a connection I could not break at will. Hanging out in the lab with me, she'd tease and flirt, laughing at the other lab assistants and the carefully serious expressions with which they'd clean rat shit off their fingers. The truth was Toni loved the lab, the perfectly square cinder-block rooms, the walls of cages, and the irritable way I'd stalk around with my broom and dustpan. She loved to follow me over in the evening to watch me sweep up the little grey turds and chopped-up computer printouts that lined the bottoms of the cages. Sipping from her omnipresent thermos of vodka and orange juice, she'd throw cashews at the bald-headed monkeys and tease me about how my ass moved when I bent over with my pan.

Once I'd gotten so angry I'd grabbed her thermos and threatened to kick her out of "my" lab.

"Oh sweetheart, you don't want me to go," she'd told me, and tried to coax me up on one of the big empty lab tables beside her.

"Have a sip. Have a little smoke. Tell me how you always wanted to find somebody like me to tease you, and love you, and suck on your nipples till you howling at the moon."

"Oh yeah. Uh huh. I just always knew some black-eyed woman was gonna come along dying to fuck me silly in front of a bunch of toothless monkeys."

"Prescient. That's what you were."

"Desperate, maybe. That's what I was when I let you talk me into bringing you over here."

"Oh, girl." She held a joint in her left hand and using her right hand only, she pulled out a match, struck it against the pack, lit the joint, took a puff, and then held it out to me.

"Have a smoke and lighten up. I'm the one on your side, you know."

Her mouth was wide and soft; the right side turned up a little in that way made my hips feel loose. Above that mouth her black eyes were shining and bright. Sometimes when I wanted to make her feel good, I would make my own eyes widen, intensify my gaze, and give her the look of love she was giving me at that moment. For me it was lust; only in her eyes did it become love. But she *was* on my side, I knew that. Toni was old school. For all that she was my age and just another scholarship student in a blue-jean jacket, she was and knew herself to be, a bar dyke with a bar dyke's studied moves, the low and sauntering strut of a great fighter and a better lover. She had, too, a bar dyke's rough and ready talent for getting me angry and then charming me out of it. Every time she played that game and made those moves, all the anger went out of me.

"Yeah," I told her, looking into her soft eyes. "You're on my side."

She drew the smoke deep into her lungs and smiled drunkenly. "Girl, girl. You act like butter wouldn't melt in your mouth. Keeping your eyes down and your voice so soft. Wearing those silly-assed sandals and damn-fool embroidered denim blouses. Always telling those drawling lies about all your cousins, and granddaddies, and uncles. . ."

"They an't lies."

"Then they should be."

"And you." She was making me angry again. "Who do you think you are?"

She pulled her legs up, ran one hand down her heavily muscled thigh, arched her back to stretch, and gave me another of her slow wandering looks, her eyes sliding up from my crotch to my face, heating my skin as she went.

"Me?" she drawled. "Me? Why, I'm just the daughter of the man with the smallest used car lot in Pinellas County and a mama who an't been sober since the day I was conceived. They wanted me to go to college and make something of myself, so here I am. Trouble is they an't got the first notion that all I really want is to be the sun and the moon and the stars to some butter-tongued girl in silly-assed sandals and an embroidered denim blouse."

"You say."

"I do indeed."

I'd laughed, not believing her, but enjoying her anyway—maybe because I didn't believe her. It was so much easier if she was not too serious, if I didn't have to think about what might happen if what was going on between us was love—love the way people talked about it, real love, dangerous and scary and not to be trusted at all. I pulled open the top snap on my blouse and trailed my fingernails up from my breasts to my throat.

"You the butter-tongued one it seems to me."

I leaned forward until my face was close to hers. She turned the joint around, tucked the lit end in her mouth, and kissed me so that the smoke shotgunned into my lungs. I melted into her ribs, pushing my hips against her thighs. She kept pushing smoke into me until the room seemed to rock unsteadily and my hands started to roam over her bunched and shaking shoulders.

Toni hadn't seemed to draw a breath through all that long speech, but when I slid into her arms she was breathless, and so was I.

"Do me." The words came out in a grating whisper. "Do me right."

"Oh, girl!" Her voice was hoarse. Her teeth raked my neck, and her fingernails tore at my ribs. My hands started shaking so bad, I couldn't get my jeans unzipped. She grabbed my wrists and pulled my hands behind my back, holding them there with one hand while she used the other to rip the snaps of my blouse open and unzip my jeans slowly. I wanted to scream "hurry," but clamped my teeth instead. If I said a word, she would just slow down and tease me more ruthlessly. I heard my sobs like they were echoes in a wind tunnel. She inched my jeans down over my butt until I was whining like a monkey strapped to a metal table.

"Oh, fuck me. Goddamn it! Fuck me!" I begged. Toni slid me to the edge of the table until my head hung off and my hair swept the floor. When her fingers opened my cunt and her teeth found my breast, I started to scream and the monkeys in the wall cages screamed with me. I jerked and pushed against her, wanting to fight, wanting to give in, wanting the world to stop and wait while I did it all. When I finally started to come, I swung my head until the cages blurred and the monkeys became red and brown shimmering cartoons. Toni climbed over me and put her naked belly against mine, and I began to cry the deepest aching sobs. It felt as if my skin itself were trying to absorb her, soak up the peace and silence inside her. I wanted to stuff myself with her until I was all cotton-battened, dark and still.

"Love," Toni whispered.

"Sex," I told myself, inside my vast quiet open body. "Sex, sex, just sex."

I was bitten as a child by a monkey—a dirty-furred, grey-faced creature kept caged by the lake where my stepfather would go on Sunday to try for a catfish dinner. That monkey was so mean she was famous for it. She had an old red collar with a bell on it, and I always wondered how anyone got close enough to her to put it on. When we'd tried to feed her sugar water from my sister's baby bottle, she'd jumped for the wire mesh walls of her cage and shrieked into my sister's terrified face. Then she'd grabbed the nipple off the bottle before any of us could pull it away, chewed it into little pieces and spit them out, swung down and grabbed handfuls of sand and fish scales from the bottom of the cage and thrown them at us. In stunned slow motion, my little sister started to blink and cry, and the monkey came up like an avenging angel to catch her long blonde hair and try to pull her through the wire mesh.

It happened so fast, I couldn't think. I put one hand flat against the cage, grabbed my sister's hair close to her scalp and set myself to fight the monkey for her. But the monkey was faster—faster and smarter. She dropped the hair and sprung against the mesh, curled little monkey claws around my wrist, and began to happily chew off my little finger while grinning up into my eyes. The man who managed the fishing camp ran over with a string of dead fish and used them to beat the monkey off. I got my hand back with a web of fine toothy slices ridging my knuckles and wrist.

The curious thing was after that, I loved that monkey. When we'd go back to the fishing camp, I'd show off my gouged and dented fingers to the other kids and boast.

"See. She ate a piece of me."

All the kids in the camp would come to see, then go over to toss fish heads and stones into her cage. They were awed and fascinated, and more than a little scared, too. The monkey, with her gnat-eaten neck and mad red eyes, shrieked and shrieked. Eventually, too many parents complained about the noise and the stink. They dropped the monkey, cage and all, into the center of the lake.

Toni loved my story of the fishing camp, said it made her Southern literature class come alive when she re-read the books in my drawl. "Trailer parks and fishing camps—that's where we growing our storytellers these days. You got possibilities, girl, as a true storyteller. Put a little work into it and you could be famous."

"Right, make a living at it, no doubt."

"Of a kind. Make some people happy anyway. You think about what a queer sort you are, girl, you and your finger-eating monkey. You Southern dirt-country types are all alike. Faulkner would have put that stuff to use, made it a literary detail. Faulkner would have had you in here spouting soliloquies to the monkeys."

Toni pulled a library book out of her backpack and tossed it in my direction. "Or Flannery O'Connor. This one's just like you, honey. She'd have given you a vision of Jesus with monkey's blood. She'd have had you chop off your own fingers and feed them to the monkeys." Toni hugged her pack to her ribs and rocked with giggles.

"Shit girl, it's just too much, too Southern Gothic—catfish and monkeys and chewed-off fingers. Throw in a little red dirt and chicken feathers, a little incest and shotgun shells, and you could join the literary tradition."

I caught her shoulder with my hand and shook her, suddenly outrageously angry. "Shit and nonsense!" I cursed, but Toni just rolled in my grip and went on laughing.

"God damn, honey. It's all nonsense, like sexual obsession— nothing to do with reality no how." She pushed my hands away and pulled her pack on.

"Remember, I'm the literature major around here. You just the anthropologist."

"Biologist. I told you I'm gonna switch over and become a biologist."

Toni shook her head indulgently. "Sure, then you're gonna settle down, marry some sweet boy, and raise mean-assed daughters to please your mama. I'll believe that when I see it."

When I didn't say anything, Toni's face took on a mock-serious expression. She reached out to the rack of cages against the wall and put her fingers to the trembling crossed wrists of a scared young monkey.

"You know," she began, "if you were to work your stories well enough, someone would be sure to conclude they had something to do with your inverted proclivities, your les-bi-an-ism. Something like you constantly re-enacting the rescue of your little sister. Hell, you could make some psychiatrist just piss his britches with excitement."

I felt my lips pull tight with anger. The monkeys chittered in their cages. "But what about you, huh? What do you believe, Miss Literary Analyst?"

"Oh, honey," she stretched her drawl, almost laughing at me. "It's got nothing to do with what I believe. I'm talking about the world, everyone outside the circle of you and me—all those professors you tell your cute little stories to and the women who come 'round to hear your lies—all those lies you don't have to tell me."

"I don't lie to you."

"Don't you?" Her laugh this time wasn't funny. "Well, never mind then. Tell me the story 'bout the fishing camp again. Tell me about that poor sad monkey you got so fond of."

Toni scratched the fur on the soft-eyed monkey in her cage, tracing a line above red-lined patient eyes. "How 'bout this one over here? Your monkey look like this one?"

"I don't remember. That was a long time ago."

"Only a moment in the mind, girl. Think about it. All those details you produce on prompting, the feel of the mesh, the stink of the fish, all that story stuff that rolls out of you so easily when you got an audience around. Bet you got that monkey in your mind all the time."

"You jealous?"

"More like you're guilty? Guilty 'bout how you play up to any and everybody, but got so little time for the folks who really care about you?"

"You, huh? You want me to believe you just live for me, huh?"

"Hell, me and the monkeys, girl. Me and the monkeys." She was teasing and she wasn't. It was the end of the semester, and for weeks she'd been trying to talk me into moving out of the dorm and into an apartment with her for the beginning of the next term.

"Think about it. We'd have a door we could lock against the world."

I thought about it. I thought about never being alone when I wanted to be, about Toni keeping track of where I went and what I did, of her sudden angers and drunken tirades. But I also thought about all those Sunday mornings lying against Toni's thigh out in front of the dormitory, reading the paper and swapping nasty stories until we were both squirming in our jeans with nowhere to go to have sex. Then I thought about making love any time I wanted until I would get to needing it, having to have it, and only Toni to provide it. I thought about getting to where I trusted her and what she might do then. A kind of terror came up from my belly and strangled me. I'd never trusted anybody in my life. How could I trust Toni?

"No," I told her. "I don't want to move in with you."

Toni's black eyes narrowed, and her left hand slapped the monkey cage, sending its captive into shrieking hysterics. "Shit, bitch. You just want your stuff taken care of and never having to trade nothing for it. You tell yourself it's just sex, and sex an't nothing but itch-scratching. You tell yourself lies, girl. You live your life on lies."

She grabbed my wrists and pulled me close to her. I pulled back, and we both almost fell. For a moment we stood close, trembling, then she threw my hands down.

"Even monkeys take mating seriously." Her anger and hurt and outrage seemed to vibrate right through me. My own anger came rolling back.

"What do you know about monkeys? What do you know about anything?"

"More than your stories, girl. More than your stories tell anyone. I know who I am. I know what I want. And I know what an't worth my trouble, what an't worth another minute of my time."

I thought she was going to slap me. I wanted her to slap me. If she slapped me, she would be the bad guy. I would be the heroine, the victim. I'd be able to stare her down and hate her forever. But she didn't touch me. She shook her hands like she was throwing off dust, turned around and walked away. It was a good move. It was the perfect dismissive bar dyke move.

I worked in the labs over the holidays, slept on a lab table, and went back to the nearly empty dorm only to shower and change my clothes. I lived on peanut butter sandwiches and Pabst Blue Ribbon beer from the cases the other lab assistants had hidden behind the furnace. The warm beer gave me gas, and I'd sit up on one of the tables and entertain the monkeys with rock-and-roll punctuated with burps. I sang the love songs the loudest, emphasizing the female pronouns by slapping the table.

The monkeys were remarkably quiet, only getting noisy if I beat the table too long. They stared at me out of infinitely wise and patient faces. I poured them all a little beer and smeared peanut butter on their feed trays. They loved the peanut butter and chewed with great wide-smacking sounds. I knew I could trust them. They wouldn't tell my secrets to anybody.

"The problem is..." I told them, checking first to be sure the door was locked. "The problem is I don't love her. I want to love her. I want to love somebody. I want to go crazy with love, eat myself up with love. Starve myself, strangle and die with love, like everybody else. Like the rest of the whole goddamned world. I want to be like the rest of the world."

I went up and put my hands flat against one of the cages. The monkey inside, old and hunched and grey, watched me with eyes that seemed to be all whites.

"But I'm not," I whispered. I was drunk, but I was telling the truth.

"I'm not like anyone else in the whole wide world. And all I want of Toni is just a little piece now and then. A little controlled piece that she won't mind giving me, that she wants to give me. You understand? I don't want nothing too serious. I don't want to need her too much. I don't want to need her at all."

Those wide blank eyes looked back at me. I could see myself in the black centers, my hair wild and uncombed around my face, my own eyes as wide as the monkey's, as blank, the pupils as black and empty as night. My mouth worked, and in the blackness I saw my own teeth—clenching, shining, grinding. My teeth scared me right down into my soul. I stole all the dimes from the petty cash drawer and called Toni from the pay phone in the dorm. She listened to me babble and made soft soothing noises into my ears.

"It's all right, baby. I understand. Don't none of us want to be too alone if we can help it, now and then."

I put the phone tight to my teeth and sobbed until she yelled to make me stop.

"If now and then's all you got to offer, then we'll see about now and then."

The last Sunday before we all went away for the summer, Toni borrowed a few hours time from a friend with an apartment in town. I'd quit my job in the lab and taken another in the post office, signed up for computer classes, and was trying to stop dreaming about plush-faced monkeys and wild red rats. Toni and I made love until we were too sore to move and then lay naked, sweating into each other's hips. Toni held my hands, fingering the two scars that remained on my right little finger. After a few minutes she sucked my fingers into her mouth and bit down gently.

"Tell me about that fishing camp again." I could barely understand her, and didn't want to talk anyway.

"No."

"That monkey left her mark on you, didn't she?"

"Only one that ever did." I looked into her eyes when I said it, knowing what I was saying as much as she did.

"Only one, huh? You think that's just?"

I shrugged, my eyes never leaving hers.

"There is no justice," I told her, meaning it, meaning it absolutely.

Toni sighed and rolled over. She took a long pull from the half-empty glass of beer she'd left on the floor, and then looked up at me from under her eyebrows.

"Tell you what," she whispered, "I want you to put me in one of your stories sometime."

I took the glass away from her, took a drink myself. "What in the world for?"

She took the glass back and turned away from me. "I want to be there," she said over her shoulder. "I just want to be there, right in there with the monkeys. Me, you understand—raw and drunk and hairy. Me, the way I am. You put me in there, huh? You just put me in there."

DON'T TELL ME YOU DON'T KNOW

I came out of the bathroom with my hair down wet on my shoulders. My Aunt Alma, my mama's oldest sister, was standing in the middle of Casey's dusty hooked rug looking like she had just flown in on it, her grey hair straggling out of its misshapen bun. For a moment I was so startled I couldn't move. Aunt Alma just stood there looking around at the big bare room with its two church pews bracketing the only other furniture—a massive pool table. I froze while the water ran down from my hair to dampen the collar of the oversized tuxedo shirt I used for a bathrobe.

"Aunt Alma," I stammered, "well...welcome...."

"You really live here?" she breathed, as if, even for me, such a situation was quite past her ability to believe. "Like this?"

I looked around as if I were seeing it for the first time myself, shrugged and tried to grin. "It's big," I offered, "lots of space, four porches, all these windows. We get along well here, might not in a smaller place." I looked back through the kitchen to Terry's room with its thick dark curtains covering a wall of windows. Empty. So was Casey's room on the other side of the kitchen. It was quiet and still, with no one even walking through the rooms overhead.

"Thank God," I whispered to myself. Nobody else was home.

Aunt Alma turned around slowly and stepped over to the mantel with the old fly-spotted mirror over it. She pushed a few of her loose hairs back and then laid her big rattan purse up by a stack of fliers Terry had left there, brushing some of the dust away first.

"My God," she echoed, "dirtier than we ever lived. Didn't think you'd turn out like this."

I shrugged again, embarrassed and angry and trying not to show it. Well hell, what could I do? I hadn't seen her in so long. She hadn't even been around that last year I'd lived with Mama, and I wasn't

sure I particularly wanted to see her now. But why was she here anyway? How had she found me?

I closed the last two buttons on my shirt and tried to shake some
of the water out of my hair. Aunt Alma watched me through the
dark spots of the mirror, her mouth set in an old familiar line. "Well,"
I said, "I didn't expect to see you." I reached up to push hair back
out of my eyes. "You want to sit down?"

Aunt Alma turned around and bumped her hip against the pool
table. "Where?" One disdainful glance rendered the pews for what
they were—exquisitely uncomfortable even for my hips. Her expression reminded me of my Uncle Jack's jokes about her, about how
she refused to go back to church till they put in rocking chairs.

"No rocking chairs here," I laughed, hoping she'd laugh with me.
Aunt Alma just leaned forward and rocked one of the balls on the
table against another. Her mouth kept its flat, impartial expression.
I tried gesturing across the pool table to my room and the big waterbed
outlined in sunlight and tree shade from the three windows over-
looking it.

"It's cleaner in there," I offered, "it's my room. This is our collective space." I gestured around.

"Collective," my aunt echoed me again, but the way she said the
word expressed clearly her opinion of such arrangements. She looked
toward my room with its narrow cluttered desk and stacks of books,
then turned back to the pool table as by far the more interesting view.
She rocked the balls again so that the hollow noise of the thump
resounded against the high, dim ceiling.

"Pitiful," she sighed, and gave me a sharp look, her washed-out
blue eyes almost angry. Two balls broke loose from the others and
rolled idly across the matted green surface of the table. The sunlight
reflecting through the oak leaves outside made Aunt Alma's face seem
younger than I remembered it, some of the hard edge eased off the
square jaw.

"Your mama is worried about you."

"I don't know why." I turned my jaw to her, knowing it would
remind her of how much alike we had always been, the people who
had said I was more her child than my mama's. "I'm fine. Mama should
know that. I spoke to her not too long ago."

"How long ago?"

I frowned, mopped at my head some more. Two months, three,
last month? "I'm not sure...Reese's birthday. I think it was Reese's
birthday."

"Three months." My aunt rocked one ball back and forth across her palm, a yellow nine ball. The light filtering into the room went a shade darker. The -9- gleamed pale through her fingers. I looked more closely at her. She looked just as she had when I was thirteen, her hair grey in that loose bun, her hands large and swollen, her body straining the seams of the faded print dress. She'd worn her hair short for a while, but it was grown long again now, and the print dress under her coat could have been any dress she'd worn in the last twenty years. She'd gotten old, suddenly, after the birth of her eighth child, but since then she seemed not to change at all. She looked now as if she would go on forever—a worn stubborn woman who didn't care what you saw when you looked at her.

I drew breath in slowly, carefully. I knew from old experience to use caution in dealing with any of my aunts, and this was the oldest and most formidable. I'd seen grown men break down and cry when she'd kept that look on them too long; little children repent and swear to change their ways. But I'd also seen my other aunts stare her right back, and like them I was a grown woman minding my own business. I had a right to look her in the eye, I told myself. I was no wayward child, no half-drunk, silly man. I was her namesake, my mama's daughter. I had to be able to look her in the eye. If I couldn't, I was in trouble, and I didn't want that kind of trouble here, 500 miles and half a lifetime away from my aunts and the power of their eyes.

Slow, slow, the balls rocked one against the other. Aunt Alma looked over at me levelly. I let the water run down between my breasts, looked back at her. My mama's sister. I could feel the tears pushing behind my eyes. It had been so long since I'd seen her or any of them! The last time I'd been to Old Henderson Road had been years back. Aunt Alma had stood on that sagging porch and looked at me, memorizing me, both of us knowing we might not see each other again. She'd moved her mouth and I'd seen the pain there, the shadow of the nephew behind her—yet another one she was raising since her youngest son, another cousin of mine, had run off and left the girl who'd birthed that boy. The pain in her eyes was achingly clear to me, the certain awful knowledge that measured all her children and wrenched her heart.

Something wrong with that boy, my uncles had laughed.

Yeah, something. Dropped on his head one too many times, you think? I think.

My aunt, like my mama, understood everything, expected nothing, and watched her own life like a terrible fable from a Sunday morning sermon. It was the perspective that all those women shared, the view that I could not, for my life, accept. I believed, I believed with all my soul that death was behind it, that death was the seed and the fruit of that numbed and numbing attitude. More than anything else, it was my anger that had driven me away from them, driven them away from me—my unpredictable, automatic anger. Their anger, their hatred, always seemed shielded, banked and secret, and because of that—shameful. My uncles were sudden, violent, and daunting. My aunts wore you down without ever seeming to fight at all. It was my anger that my aunts thought queer, my wild raging temper they respected in a boy and discouraged in a girl. That I slept with girls was curious, but not dangerous. That I slept with a knife under my pillow and refused to step aside for my uncles was more than queer. It was crazy.

Aunt Alma's left eye twitched, and I swallowed my tears, straightened my head, and looked her full in the face. I could barely hold myself still, barely return her look. Again those twin emotions, the love and the outrage that I'd always felt for my aunt, warred in me. I wanted to put out my hand and close my fingers on her hunched, stubborn shoulder. I wanted to lay my head there and pull tight to her, but I also wanted to hit her, to scream and kick and make her ashamed of herself. Nothing was clean between us, especially not our love.

Between my mama and Aunt Alma there were five other sisters. The most terrible and loved was Bess, the one they swore had always been so smart. From the time I was eight Aunt Bess had a dent in the left side of her head—a shadowed dent that emphasized the twitch of that eye, just like the twitch Aunt Alma has, just like the twitch I sometimes get, the one they tell me is nerves. But Aunt Bess wasn't born with that twitch as we were, just as she wasn't born with that dent. My uncle, her husband, had come up from the deep dust on the road, his boots damp from the river, picking up clumps of dust and making mud, knocking it off on her steps, her screen door, her rug, the back rung of a kitchen chair. She'd shouted at him, "Not on my clean floor!" and he'd swung the bucket, river-stained and heavy with crawfish. He'd hit her in the side of the head—dented her into a lifetime of stupidity and half-blindness. Son of a bitch never even said he was sorry, and all my childhood he'd laughed at her, the way she'd sometimes stop in the middle of a sentence and grope painfully for a word.

None of *them* had told me that story. I had been grown and out of the house before one of the Greenwood cousins had told it so I understood, and as much as I'd hated him then, I'd raged at them more.

"You let him live?" I'd screamed at them. "He did that to her and you did nothing! You did nothing to him, nothing for her."

"What'd you want us to do?"

My Aunt Grace had laughed at me. "You want us to cut him up and feed him to the river? What good would that have done her or her children?"

She'd shaken her head, and they had all stared at me as if I were still a child and didn't understand the way the world was. The cold had gone through me then, as if the river were running up from my bowels. I'd felt my hands curl up and reach, but there was nothing to reach for. I'd taken hold of myself, my insides, and tried desperately to voice the terror that was tearing at me.

"But to leave her with him after he did that, to just let it stand, to let him get away with it." I'd reached and reached, trying to get to them, to make them feel the wave moving up and through me. "It's like all of it, all you let them get away with."

"Them?" My mama had watched my face as if afraid of what she might find there. "Who do you mean? And what do you think we could do?"

I couldn't say it. I'd stared into mama's face, and looked from her to all of them, to those wide, sturdy cheekbones, those high, proud eyebrows, those set and terrible mouths. I had always thought of them as mountains, mountains that everything conspired to grind but never actually broke. The women of my family were all I had ever believed in. What was I if they were not what I had shaped them in my own mind? All I had known was that I had to get away from them—all of them—the men who could do those terrible things and the women who would let it happen to you. I'd never forgiven any of them.

It might have been more than three months since I had talked to Mama on the telephone. It had been far longer than that since I had been able to really talk to any of them. The deepest part of me didn't believe that I would ever be able to do so. I dropped my eyes and pulled myself away from Aunt Alma's steady gaze. I wanted to reach for her, touch her, maybe cry with her, if she'd let me.

"People will hurt you more with pity than with hate," she'd always told me. "I can hate back, or laugh at them, but goddamn the son of a bitch that hands me pity."

No pity. Not allowed. I reached to rock a ball myself.

"Want to play?" I tried looking up into her eyes again. It was too close. Both of us looked away.

"I'll play myself." She set about racking up the balls. Her mouth was still set in that tight line. I dragged a kitchen stool in and sat in the doorway out of her way, telling myself I had to play this casually, play this as family, and wait and see what the point was.

"Where's Uncle Bill?" I was rubbing my head again and trying to make conversation.

"What do you care? I don't think Bill said ten words to you in your whole life." She rolled the rack forward and back, positioning it perfectly for the break. " 'Course he didn't say many more to anybody else either." She grinned, not looking at me, talking as if she were pouring tea at her own kitchen table. "Nobody can say I married that man for his conversation."

She leaned into her opening shot, and I leaned forward in appreciation. She had a great stance, her weight centered over her massive thighs. My family runs to heavy women, gravy-fed working women, the kind usually seen in pictures taken at mining disasters. Big women, all of my aunts move under their own power and stalk around telling everybody else what to do. But Aunt Alma was the prototype, the one I had loved most, starting back when she had given us free meals in the roadhouse she'd run for a while. It had been one of those bad times when my stepfather had been out of work and he and Mama were always fighting. Mama would load us all in the Pontiac and crank it up on seventy-five cents worth of gas, just enough to get to Aunt Alma's place on the Eustis Highway. Once there, we'd be fed on chicken gravy and biscuits, and Mama would be fed from the well of her sister's love and outrage.

You tell that bastard to get his ass out on the street. Whining don't make money. Cursing don't get a job...

Bitching don't make the beds and screaming don't get the tomatoes planted. They had laughed together then, speaking a language of old stories and older jokes.

You tell him.

I said.

Now girl, you listen to me.

The power in them, the strength and the heat! How could anybody not love my mama, my aunts? How could my daddy, my uncles, ever stand up to them, dare to raise hand or voice to them? They were a power on the earth.

I breathed deep, watching my aunt rock on her stance, settling her eye on the balls, while I smelled chicken gravy and hot grease, the close thick scent of love and understanding. I used to love to eat at Aunt Alma's house, all those home-cooked dinners at the road-house; pinto beans with peppers for fifteen, nine of them hers. Chow-chow on a clean white plate passed around the table while the biscuits passed the other way. My aunt always made biscuits. What else stretched so well? Now those starch meals shadowed her loose shoulders and dimpled her fat white elbows.

She gave me one quick glance and loosed her stroke. The white ball punched the center of the table. The balls flew to the edges. My sixty-year-old aunt gave a grin that would have scared piss out of my Uncle Bill, a grin of pure, fierce enjoyment. She rolled the stick in fingers loose as butter on a biscuit, laughed again, and slid her palms down the sides of polished wood, while the anger in her face melted into skill and concentration.

I rocked back on my stool and covered my smile with my wet hair. Goddamn! Aunt Alma pushed back on one ankle, swung the stick to follow one ball, another, dropping them as easily as peas on potatoes. Goddamn! She went after those balls like kids on a dirt yard, catching each lightly and dropping them lovingly. Into the holes, move it! Turning and bracing on ankles thickened with too many years of flour and babies, Aunt Alma blitzed that table like a twenty-year-old hustler, not sparing me another glance.

Not till the eighth stroke did she pause and stop to catch her breath.

"You living like this—not for a man, huh?" she asked, one eyebrow arched and curious.

"No," I shrugged, feeling more friendly and relaxed. Moving like that, aunt of mine I wanted to say, don't tell me you don't understand.

"Your mama said you were working in some photo shop, doing shit work for shit money. Not much to show for that college degree, is that?"

"Work is work. It pays the rent."

"Which ought not to be much here."

"No," I agreed, "not much. I know," I waved my hands lightly, "it's a wreck of a place, but it's home. I'm happy here. Terry, Casey and everybody—they're family."

"Family." Her mouth hardened again. "You have a family, don't you remember? These girls might be close, might be important to you, but they're not family. You know that." Her eyes said more, much more. Her eyes threw the word *family* at me like a spear. All her longing, all her resentment of my abandonment was in that word, and not only hers, but Mama's and my sisters' and all the cousins' I had carefully not given my new address.

"How about a beer?" I asked. I wanted one myself. "I've got a can of Pabst in the icebox."

"A glass of water," she said. She leaned over the table to line up her closing shots.

I brought her a glass of water. "You're good," I told her, wanting her to talk to me about how she had learned to play pool, anything but family and all this stuff I so much did not want to think about.

"Children," she stared at me again. "What about children?" There was something in her face then that waited, as if no question were more important, as if she knew the only answer I could give.

Enough, I told myself, and got up without a word to get myself that can of Pabst. I did not look in her eyes. I walked into the kitchen on feet that felt suddenly unsteady and tender. Behind me, I heard her slide the cue stick along the rim of the table and then draw it back to set up another shot.

Play it out, I cursed to myself, just play it out and leave me alone. Everything is so simple for you, so settled. Make babies. Grow a garden. Handle some man like he's just another child. Let everything come that comes, die that dies; let everything go where it goes. I drank straight from the can and watched her through the doorway. All my uncles were drunks, and I was more like them than I had ever been like my aunts.

Aunt Alma started talking again, walking around the table, measuring shots and not even looking in my direction. "You remember when ya'll lived out on Greenlake Road? Out on that dirt road where that man kept that old egg-busting dog? Your mama couldn't keep a hen to save her life till she emptied a shell and filled it again with chicken shit and baby piss. Took that dog right out of himself when he ate it. Took him right out of the taste for hens and eggs." She stopped to take a deep breath, sweat glittering on her lip. With one hand she wiped it away, the other going white on the pool cue.

"I still had Annie then. Lord, I never think about her anymore."

I remembered then the last child she had borne, a tiny girl with a heart that fluttered with every breath, a baby for whom the doctors said nothing could be done, a baby they swore wouldn't see six months. Aunt Alma had kept her in an okra basket and carried her everywhere, talking to her one minute like a kitten or a doll and the next minute like a grown woman. Annie had lived to be four, never outgrowing the vegetable basket, never talking back, just lying there and smiling like a wise old woman, dying between a smile and a laugh while Aunt Alma never interrupted the story that had almost made Annie laugh.

I sipped my beer and watched my aunt's unchanging face. Very slowly she swung the pool cue up and down, not quite touching the table. After a moment she stepped in again and leaned half her weight on the table. The 5-ball became a bird murdered in flight, dropping suddenly into the far right pocket.

Aunt Alma laughed out loud, delighted. "Never lost it," she crowed. "Four years in the roadhouse with that table set up in the back. Every one of them sons of mine thought he was going to make money on it. Lord those boys! Never made a cent." She swallowed the rest of her glass of water.

"But me," she wiped the sweat away again. "I never would have done it for money. I just loved it. Never went home without playing myself three or four games. Sometimes I'd set Annie up on the side and we'd pretend we was playing. I'd tell her when I was taking her shots. And she'd shout when I'd sink 'em. I let her win most every time."

She stopped, put both hands on the table, closed her eyes.

" 'Course, just after we lost her, we lost the roadhouse." She shook her head, eyes still closed. "Never did have anything fine that I didn't lose."

The room was still, dust glinted in the sunlight past her ears. She opened her eyes and looked directly at me.

"I don't care," she began slowly, softly. "I don't care if you're queer or not. I don't care if you take puppydogs to bed, for that matter, but your mother was all my heart for twenty years when nobody else cared what happened to me. She stood by me. I've stood by her and I always thought to do the same for you and yours. But she's sitting there, did you know that? She's sitting there like nothing's left of her life, like. . .like she hates her life and won't say shit to nobody about it. She wouldn't tell me. She won't tell me what it is, what has happened."

I sat the can down on the stool, closed my own eyes, dropped my head. I didn't want to see her. I didn't want her to be there. I wanted her to go away, disappear out of my life the way I'd run out of hers. Go away, old woman. Leave me alone. Don't talk to me. Don't tell me your stories. I an't a baby in a basket, and I can't lie still for it.

"You know. You know what it is. The way she is about you. I

know it has to be you—something about you. I want to know what
it is, and you're going to tell me. Then you're going to come home
with me and straighten this out. There's a lot I an't never been able
to fix, but this time, this thing, I'm going to see it out. I'm going to
see it fixed."

I opened my eyes and she was still standing there, the cue stick
shiny in her hand, her face all flushed and tight.

"Go," I said and heard my voice, a scratchy, strangling cry in the
big room. "Get out of here."

"What did you tell her? What did you say to your mama?"

"Ask her. Don't ask me. I don't have nothing to say to you."

The pool cue rose slowly, slowly till it touched the right cheek,
the fine lines of broken blood vessels, freckles, and patchy skin. She
shook her head slowly. My throat pulled tighter and tighter until it
drew my mouth down and open. Like a shot the cue swung. The
table vibrated with the blow. Her cheeks pulled tight, the teeth all
a grimace. The cue split and broke. White dust rose in a cloud. The
echo hurt my ears while her hands rose up as fists, the broken cue
in her right hand as jagged as the pain in her face.

"Don't you say that to me. Don't you treat me like that. Don't
you know who I am, what I am to you? I didn't have to come up
here after you. I could have let it run itself out, let it rest on your
head the rest of your life, just let you carry it—your mama's life. YOUR
MAMA'S LIFE, GIRL. Don't you understand me? I'm talking about
your mama's life."

She threw the stick down, turned away from me, her shoulders
heaving and shaking, her hands clutching nothing. "I an't talking
about your stepfather. I an't talking about no man at all. I'm talking
about your mama sitting at her kitchen table, won't talk to nobody,
won't eat, won't listen to nothing. What'd she ever ask from you?
Nothing. Just gave you your life and everything she had. Worked herself ugly for you and your sister. Only thing she ever hoped for was
to do the same for your children, someday to sit herself back and
hold her grandchildren on her lap. . . ."

It was too much. I couldn't stand it.

"GODDAMN YOU!" I was shaking all over. "CHILDREN! All
you ever talk about—you and her and all of you. Like that was the
end-all and be-all of everything. Never mind what happens to them
once they're made. That don't matter. It's only the getting of them.
Like some goddamned crazy religion. Get your mother a grandchild
and solve all her problems. Get yourself a baby and forget everything

else. It's what you were born for, the one thing you can do with no thinking about it at all. Only I can't. To get her a grandchild, I'd have to steal one!"

I was wringing my own hands, twisting them together and pulling them apart. Now I swung them open and slapped down at my belly, making my own hollow noise in the room.

"No babies in there, aunt of mine, and never going to be. I'm sterile as a clean tin can. That's what I told Mama, and not to hurt her. I told her because she wouldn't leave me alone about it. Like you, like all of you, always talking about children, never able to leave it alone." I was walking back and forth now, unable to stop myself from talking. "Never able to hear me when I warned her to leave it be. Going on and on till I thought I'd lose my mind."

I looked her in the eye, loving her and hating her, and not wanting to speak, but hearing the words come out anyway. "Some people never do have babies, you know. Some people get raped at eleven by a stepfather their mama half-hates but can't afford to leave. Some people then have to lie and hide it 'cause it would make so much trouble. So nobody will know, not the law and not the rest of the family. Nobody but the women supposed to be the ones who take care of everything, who know what to do and how to do it, the women who make children who believe in them and trust in them, and sometimes die for it. Some people never go to a doctor and don't find out for ten years that the son of a bitch gave them some goddamned disease."

I looked away, unable to stand how grey her face had gone.

"You know what it does to you when the people you love most in the world, the people you believe in—cannot survive without believing in—when those people do nothing, don't even know something needs to be done? When you cannot hate them but cannot help yourself? The hatred grows. It just takes over everything, eats you up and makes you somebody full of hate."

I stopped. The roar that had been all around me stopped, too. The cold was all through me now. I felt like it would never leave me. I heard her move. I heard her hip bump the pool table and make the balls rock. I heard her turn and gather up her purse. I opened my eyes to see her moving toward the front door. That cold cut me then like a knife in fresh slaughter. I knew certainly that she'd go back and take care of Mama, that she'd never say a word, probably never tell anybody she'd been here. 'Cause then she'd have to talk about the other thing, and I knew as well as she that however much she tried to forget it, she'd really always known. She'd done nothing then. She'd do nothing now. There was no justice. There was no justice in the world.

When I started to cry it wasn't because of that. It wasn't because of babies or no babies, or pain that was so far past I'd made it a source of strength. It wasn't even that I'd hurt her so bad, hurt Mama when I didn't want to. I cried because of the things I hadn't said, didn't know how to say, cried most of all because behind everything else there was no justice for my aunts or my mama. Because each of them to save their lives had tried to be strong, had become, in fact, as strong and determined as life would let them. I and all their children had believed in that strength, had believed in them and their ability to do anything, fix anything, survive anything. None of us had ever been able to forgive ourselves that we and they were not strong enough, that strength itself was not enough.

Who can say where that strength ended, where the world took over and rolled us all around like balls on a pool table? None of us ever would. I brought my hands up to my neck and pulled my hair around until I clenched it in my fists, remembering how my aunt used to pick up Annie to rub that baby's belly beneath her chin— Annie bouncing against her in perfect trust. Annie had never had to forgive her mama anything.

"Aunt Alma, wait. Wait!"

She stopped in the doorway, her back trembling, her hands gripping the doorposts. I could see the veins raised over her knuckles, the cords that stood out in her neck, the flesh as translucent as butter beans cooked until the skins come loose. Talking to my mama over the phone, I had not been able to see her face, her skin, her stunned and haunted eyes. If I had been able to see her, would I have ever said those things to her?

"I'm sorry."

She did not look back. I let my head fall back, rolled my shoulders to ease the painful clutch of my own muscles. My teeth hurt. My ears stung. My breasts felt hot and swollen. I watched the light as it moved on her hair.

"I'm sorry. I would. . .I would. . .anything. If I could change things, if I could help. . . ."

I stopped. Tears were running down my face. My aunt turned to me, her wide pale face as wet as mine. "Just come home with me. Come home for a little while. Be with your mama a little while. You don't have to forgive her. You don't have to forgive anybody. You just have to love her the way she loves you. Like I love you. Oh girl, don't you know how we love you!"

I put my hands out, let them fall apart on the pool table. My aunt was suddenly across from me, reaching across the table, taking my hands, sobbing into the cold dirty stillness—an ugly sound, not softened by the least self-consciousness. When I leaned forward, she leaned to me and our heads met, her grey hair against my temple brightened by the sunlight pouring in the windows.

"Oh, girl! Girl, you are our precious girl."

I cried against her cheek, and it was like being five years old again in the roadhouse, with Annie's basket against my hip, the warmth in the room purely a product of the love that breathed out from my aunt and my mama. If they were not mine, if I was not theirs, who was I? I opened my mouth, put my tongue out, and tasted my aunt's cheek and my own. Butter and salt, dust and beer, sweat and stink, flesh of my flesh.

"Precious," I breathed back to her.

"Precious."

DEMON LOVER

Katy always said she wanted to be the Demon Lover, the one we desire even when we know it is not us she wants, but our souls. When she comes back to me now, she comes in that form and I never fail to think that the shadows at her shoulders could be wings.

She comes in when I am not quite asleep and brings me fully awake by laying cold fingers on my warm back. Her pale skin gleams in the moonlight, reflecting every beam like a mirror of smoked glass while her teeth and nails shine phosphorescent.

"Wake up," Katy whispers, and leans over to bite my naked shoulder. "Wake up. Wake up!"

"No," I say, "not you."

But I knew she was coming. I could hear her echoes peeling back off the moments, the way Aunt Raylene always said she could hear a spell coming on. Katy's persistent. Some of my ghosts are so faded; they only come when I reach for them. This one reaches for me.

"Sit up," she says. "I won't bite you." But her teeth are sharp in the pale light, and I sit up warily. The only predictable thing about Katy was her stubborn perversity; she would mostly do whatever she swore solemnly she would not.

"Shit," I whisper, and roll over. She laughs and passes me a joint. The smoke wreathes her like a cloak, heavy and sweet around us. I inhale deeply, grin up at her and say, "My hallucinations get me stoned."

"Lucky you. It costs everyone else money."

She blows smoke out her nose. Katy has a matter-of-fact manner about her tonight, very unlike herself. It's been three years since she O.D.'d, and in that time she's grown more urgent, not less. This strange air of calmness disturbs me. If the dead lose their restlessness, do they finally go away?

Something falls in the other room, wood striking wood. It's probably Molly going to the bathroom a little drunk as usual, knocking
things over. Katy slides up on one knee and clutches the edge of the
waterbed frame. If she were a cat her hair would be on end. As it
is, the hair above her ears seems suddenly fuller. I reach over and
take the joint from her hand, moving gently, carefully soothing her
with only my unspoken demand to hold her.

"You going to wake me up in the night," I tell her, "you might
as well entertain me. Tell me where you got this delicacy. It's mashed
pecan, right? Tastes just like that batch we got in Atlanta that time
we hitchhiked up from Daytona Beach."

Still in her cat's aspect, Katy looks back at me, her huge eyes
cold and ruthless. Her expression makes me want to push into her
breast, put my tongue to her throat, and hear her cruel, lovely laugh
again. It would be easy, delicious and easy, and not at all the way
it had been when she was alive. Alive, she was never easy.

"You an't got no taste at all. It's Panama City home-grown." She
comes back down on the bed, not disturbing the mattress. "You always talking 'bout that mashed pecan, but first time I got you really
stoned on it, you got sick. Spent the night in the bathroom being
the most pitiful child. I swear."

"That was Tampa, and that killer Jamaican." I draw another deep
lungful of the sweet smoke. "In Atlanta, you got sick and threw up
on the only clean shirt I had with me."

Katy gives her laugh finally, and predictably, I feel the goosebumps
rise on my thighs. She settles herself so that her naked left hip is
against my shoulder. Her skin is smooth, cool, wonderful. I put my
hand on her thigh, and she leans forward to sniff my cheek and rub
her lips on my eyebrows. I cannot touch Katy without remembering
making love to her on Danny's couch with a dozen drunk and stoned
people around the corner in the living room; the tickle of the feathers
she wore laced into the small braids over her ears, and the cold chill
of the knife she always pulled out of her boot and pushed under the
pillows, the sheathed blade that always seemed to migrate down to
the small of my back.

Most of all I remember the talent with which Katy would bite
me just hard enough to make me gasp, her bubbling laughter as she
whispered, "Don't make no noise. They'll hear." Even now, after all
this time, I sometimes make love holding my breath, trying to make
no sound, pretending that it is the way it always was back then, with
drunk and dangerous strangers around the corner and Katy playing

at trying to get me to make a sound they might hear. It was the worst
sex and the best, the most dangerous and absolutely the most satisfying. No one else has ever made love to me like that—as if sex were
a contest on which your life depended. No one has ever scared me
so much, or made me love them so much. And no one else has ever
died on me the way she did, with everything between us unsettled
and aching.

I slap her thigh brusquely, pushing her back. "You should have
had the consideration to puke into a pot. Ruining that shirt that way.
You were always careless of me and my stuff."

Katy nods. "A little. Yeah, I was." She settles back on the mattress, crosslegged and still just touching my shoulder. "But I always
made it up to you. Remember, I stole you another shirt in Atlanta."
Her hand trading the joint is transparent. I can see right through
to her smoky breasts, the nipples dark and stiff. "That cotton cowboy shirt with the yellow yoke and the green embroidery. Made you
look like a toked-up Loretta Lynn." She gives her short, barking laugh.

"You still got that one?"

"No, I lost it somewhere."

I remember going home for the service one of the local drug coun-
selors organized. People were standing around talking about the shame
and the waste, and Katy's mama slapped my hand when I touched
her accidentally. "It should have been you," she'd hissed. "Any one
of you, it should have been. Not Katy." Her eyes had been flat and
dry. She hadn't cried at all, and neither had I. I spent that night in
my mama's kitchen, talking long distance to my lover up north about
how everybody had looked, the way Katy's last boyfriend had glared
at me from beside his parole officer. I'd hugged the phone to my ear,
that yellow cowboy shirt between my fists, wringing it until I was
shredding the yoke, pulling the snaps off, ripping the seams. I'd torn
that shirt apart, talked for hours, but had never gotten around to
crying. I didn't cry until months later in the Women's Center bathroom. I'd been stone sober, but I was standing up to piss, my knees
slightly bent, my jeans down around my ankles, my head turned to
the side so I could see myself in the mirror. It was the way Katy had
insisted we piss when we went road-tripping.

"You're the dyke," she'd always said. "Keep your health. Learn
to piss like a boy and keep your butt dry."

"Piss like a boy," I'd whispered into the mirror, into Katy's painful memory. And just that easy her face was there, her full swollen
mouth mocking me, whispering back, "Like a dyke. You the dyke

here, girl. I sure an't."

So then I'd cried, sobbed and cried, and beaten on that mirror with my fists until the women outside came to try and see what was going on. I'd shut up, washed my face and told them nothing. What could I tell them anyway? My ghost lover just came back and made me piss all over my jeans. My ghost lover is haunting me, and the trick is I am glad to see her.

Katy hands me the joint again, moving her small hands delicately. She smiles when she sees where my glance is trained. She flexes her fist, opens the fingers, and wags them in front of my nose. I laugh and take the joint again.

"I loved that shirt. It was the best present you ever got me."

"You forgetting those black gloves with the rhinestones on the back I got in that shop on Peachtree Street. We always got the best stuff in Atlanta. Didn't we?"

"You just about got us busted in Atlanta."

"Oh hell, you were just a nervous nelly. Thought you were the only woman capable of sleight of hand. You just never trusted me, girl."

"You were always so stoned. You did stupid things."

"I did wonderful things. I did amazing things, and stoned only made me better, made me smoother. Loosened me up and made me psychic. I was doing acid when I got you those gloves. That window-pane Blackie sold us."

"Purple haze. You always talk about the windowpane, but we only did it once. You talk about the windowpane 'cause you like to scare people with the notion of you sticking it in your eyes."

"I only did it once with you. I did it lots with Mickey. We put it in our eyes, in our noses. Son of a bitch even shoved it up my ass."

She crushes the joint out on the bedframe. She is smiling and relaxed now, very beautiful even though I am getting angry. Mickey was the one took her to California after I ran off. Mickey was the one got her back on junk, left her in the motel room where she overdosed. Mickey was the one threatened me at her memorial service, with his parole officer standing right there sweating in the heat. Mickey was the one I'd told to try it.

Come for me asshole, and I'll cut off your balls and push them up your butt. The parole officer had smiled, and my sweat had turned cold on my back. That wasn't like me, wasn't the kind of thing I'd say. It wasn't even the thing I'd been thinking. It was as if Katy had pushed the words out of my mouth. It was exactly the kind of thing Katy would have said.

But Mickey had overdosed himself at Raiford, and I'd never seen any of Katy's boyfriends again. Just Katy, any time she gets restless and wants to come back. I look at her now and my throat closes up. I cannot make casual conversation, cannot talk at all. I want to reach for her but I am too afraid. She is the vampire curse in my life. You have to invite them back, and part of me always wants her, even when most of me doesn't. Right now all of me wants her, flesh and blood, body and soul.

Katy's thick black eyebrows raise and lower, seeing right through me, seeing my grief and my lust. "Ahhh, bitch," she whispers, and it sounds like *lover*. She slips one hand under the sheet and strokes her nails along my leg.

I catch my breath. I could cry but don't. Will we be lovers again? Is she real enough this moment to put her filmy body along my too-tight muscles? She wants to; it shows in the unaccustomed softness in her face. I feel tears run down my cheeks.

Now she says it. "Lover."

"Junkie." I hiss it at her, beginning to really cry, making a hoarse ugly sound in the quiet room. "Goddamn you, you goddamned junkie!"

"Ahh well," she drawls, her fingers still stroking my leg. "It's not a lie." She drags herself over, rocking the bed this time, sliding under the sheet. She arranges her body to cup my side, her toes touch my ankle and her head turns so that her mouth is close to my ear.

"Not a lie, no." One hand caresses my stomach; the other hugs my hipbone.

"Goddamn you!" I try to lie still but start shaking.

"Don't be boring," she says. I feel her tongue licking my cheek, wet and almost as rough as a cat's tongue. My whole body goes stiff, and my hands ball up into fists.

"Why do you keep coming back? Why don't you leave me alone? You weren't worth the trouble when you were alive and you sure aren't doing me any good now." I start to fight her, trying to pull away or push her away. But she is smoke only, a cloud on my skin, and I can't escape her.

"Motherfucker. . . ." I give it up to cry and turn my face into the pillow of her hair. It smells so sweet and familiar, marijuana and patchouli.

Katy's shoulders ride up and down. She arches her back and slides her body over so that her belly is on top of mine. I almost scream from the intensity of the sensation. It feels so good. It feels so awful.

"You loved me." She says it right into the hollow of my ear. "You love me still. Even after you left me, you loved me. You couldn't stand me, and you damn sure couldn't save me. But you couldn't stand it without me either. So here I am. Feel me."

She drums her knuckles on my hipbone. Her teeth nip my neck. I gasp and arch up into her. "I'm part of you," she whispers. "Right down in the core of you."

I pull myself back down and lie still, giving it up. "I know." I push my face up. My mouth covers her, tastes her. Her tongue is bitter honey, sliding between my lips, filling my mouth, pushing my own tongue up to the roof of my mouth, expanding until I think I will choke. But I do not fight. I take her in. I want to swallow her, all of her. If she is a ghost, then why not? She could melt into my bones. We could be the same creature.

My hips begin to rock. My fingers curl up and try to grip her waist. A heated sweat rises all over my body. I want to rise up like steam into her, pull up right off my own bones, become something in the air, a scent of marijuana and patchouli, something sweet and nasty and impossibly sad. But I cannot get hold of her. My very movements seem to push her up and away, the cloud of her becoming mistlike, gossamer and fading.

"No!"

Her thumb is in the hollow of my throat. My own pulse roars in my ears. Her laughter is soft, too soft.

"Stop," she says, and it comes from very far away. Too far. "You'll make yourself sick."

"I'll take a pill."

"Junkie." She laughs again. Her pleasure in being able to say that to me almost makes me laugh back. "You take too many pills."

That is too much. I go limp again and look up into her black, black eyes. "Oh, mama," I giggle.

"Ooooh, maaamaaaa." Her mouth draws the words out delightfully, rich with lust. She rocks against me, and I can feel her, the flesh hard and cold and powerful.

"I'll make it interesting for both of us," she promises. Her nails rake me lightly. Goosebumps radiate from every burning pinprick. I am not afraid. I burn. I want her so badly. Like a madwoman, I don't care anymore what is real.

"You move," she tells me, "and I'm gone." The cloud of her lifts and it is all I can do to hold myself still until she comes back down. "You must hold yourself absolutely still. Absolutely."

Her skin burns me where it touches. I stiffen, holding myself for her. Her weight comes down until I shudder with pleasure. Instantly her body lifts, becomes again a cloud. Her phantom laughter is rich and close. I bite my lips and hold myself still again. She comes down again. So cold. So hot. I groan. She lifts, laughs, rises again. It goes on and on.

Do you love me? Do you want me? Do you remember me? Do you hate me? Do you love me? I love you, love you, lover you, come all over you, come up into the dark of you, the pit of you. Pull me down into the pit of you. Memory and touch and taste. You are never alone, never going to be alone. If you cry, I will. If you scream, I will. If you are, I am.

"I love you," she says.

I am drifting. I have come so much my bones have turned to concrete. Their weight immobilizes me. Katy's hot skin presses all over me. It is so dark, so still. It is the pit of the night, and I am drifting off into sleep. I want to wrap my arms around her and pull her down with me, sleep in the luxury of her embrace. But hours of conditioning stop me, and I do not move. I just slide further down into sleep. She says it again.

"I love you."

"You're dead," I mumble.

Her weight increases, presses down on me. I open my eyes.

"Doesn't matter." She has spread out, filled the room. She is enormous, masses of dark all around me. I am afraid. Suddenly I am deeply, deeply afraid, and when she laughs I feel the cold.

"Doesn't matter at all."

HER THIGHS

I was thinking about Bobby, remembering her sitting, smoking, squint-eyed, and me looking down at the way her thighs shaped in her jeans. I have always loved women in blue jeans, worn jeans, worn particularly in that way that makes the inseam fray, and Bobby's seams had that fine white sheen that only comes after long restless evenings spent jiggling one's thighs one against the other, the other against the bar stool.

After a year as my sometimes lover, Bobby's nerves were wearing as thin as her seams. She always seemed to be looking to the other women in the bar, checking out their eyes to see if, in fact, they thought her as pussy-whipped as she thought herself, for the way she could not seem to finally settle me down to playing the wife I was supposed to be. Bobby was a wild-eyed woman, proud of her fame for running women ragged—all the women who had fallen in love with her and followed her around long after she had lost all interest in them. Hanging out at softball games on lazy spring afternoons, Bobby would look over at me tossing my head and talking to some other woman and grind her thighs together in impatience. The woman was as profoundly uncomfortable with my sexual desire as my determined independence. But nothing so disturbed her as the idea other people could see both in the way I tossed my hair, swung my hips, and would not always come when she called. Bobby believed lust was a trashy lower-class impulse, and she so wanted to be nothing like that. It meant the one tool she could have used to control me was the very one she could not let herself use.

Oh, Bobby loved to fuck me. Bobby loved to beat my ass, but it bothered her that we both enjoyed it so much. Early on in our relationship, she established a pattern of having me over for the evening and strictly enforcing a rule against sex outside the bedroom.

Bobby wanted dinner—preferably Greek or Chinese take-out—and at least two hours of television. Then there had to be a bath, bath powder and toothbrushing, though she knew I prefered her unbathed and gritty, tasting of the tequila she sipped through dinner. I was not supposed to touch her until we entered the sanctuary of her bedroom, that bedroom lit only by the arc lamp in the alley outside. Only in that darkness could I bite and scratch and call her name. Only in that darkness would Bobby let herself open to passion.

Let me set the scene for you, me in my hunger for her great strong hands and perfect thighs, and her in her deliberate disregard. When feeling particularly cruel, Bobby would even insist on doing her full twenty-minute workout while I lay on the bed tearing at the sheets with my nails. I was young, unsure of myself, and so I put up with it, sometimes even enjoyed it, though what I truly wanted was her in a rage, under spotlights in a stadium, fucking to the cadence of a lesbian rock-and-roll band.

But it was years ago, and if I was too aggressive, she wouldn't let me touch her. So I waited, and watched her, and calculated. I'd start my efforts on the couch, finding excuses to play with her thighs. Rolling joints and reaching over to drop a few shreds on her lap, I scrambled for every leaf on her jeans.

"Don't want to waste any," I told her, and licked my fingers to catch the fine grains that caught in her seams. I progressed to stroking her crotch. "For the grass," I said, going on to her inseam, her knees, the backs of her thighs.

"Perhaps some slipped under here, honey. Let me see."

I got her used to the feel of my hands legitimately wandering, while her eyes never left the TV screen. I got her used to the heat of my palms, the slight scent of the sweat on my upper lip, the firm pressure of my wrists sliding past her hips. I was as calculated as any woman who knows what she wants, but I cannot tell you what magic I used to finally get her to sit still for me going down on my knees and licking that denim.

It wasn't through begging. Bobby recognized begging as a sexual practice, therefore to be discouraged outside the darkened bedroom. I didn't wrestle her for it. That, too, was allowed only in the bedroom. Bobby was the perfect withholding butch, I tell you, so I played the perfect compromising femme. I think what finally got to her was the tears.

Keeping my hands on her, I stared at her thighs intently until she started that sawing motion—crossing and recrossing her legs. My impudence made her want to grab and shake me, but that, too, might have been sex, so she couldn't. Bobby shifted and cleared her throat and watched me while I kept my mouth open slightly and stared intently at the exact spot where I wanted to put my tongue. My eyes were full of moisture. I imagined touching the denim above her labia with my lips. I saw it so clearly, her taste and texture were full in my mouth. I got wet and wetter. Bobby kept shifting on the couch. I felt my cheeks dampen and heard myself making soft moaning noises—like a young child in great hunger. That strong, dark musk odor rose between us, the smell that comes up from my cunt when I am swollen and wet from my clit to my asshole.

Bobby smelled it. She looked at my face, and her cheeks turned the brightest pink. I felt momentarily like a snake who has finally trapped a rabbit. Caught like that, on the living room couch, all her rules were momentarily suspended. Bobby held herself perfectly still, except for one moment when she put her blunt fingers on my left cheek. I leaned over and licked delicately at the seam on first the left and then the right inner thigh. Her couch was one of those swollen chintz monsters, and my nose would bump the fabric each time I moved from right to left. I kept bumping it, moving steadily, persistently, not touching her with any other part of my body except my tongue. Under her jeans, her muscles rippled and strained as if she were holding off a great response or reaching for one. I felt an extraordinary power. I had her. I knew absolutely that I was in control.

Oh, but it was control at a cost, of course, or I would be there still. I could hold her only by calculation, indirection, distraction. It was dear, that cost, and too dangerous. I had to keep a distance in my head, an icy control on my desire to lose control. I wanted to lay the whole length of my tongue on her, to dribble over my chin, to flatten my cheeks to that fabric and shake my head on her seams like a dog on a fine white bone. But that would have been too real, too raw. Bobby would never have sat still for that. I held her by the unreality of my hunger, my slow nibbling civilized tongue.

Oh, Bobby loved that part of it, like she loved her chintz sofa, the antique armoire with the fold-down shelf she used for a desk, the carefully balanced display of appropriate liquors she never touched —unlike the bottles on the kitchen shelves she emptied and replaced weekly. Bobby loved the aura of acceptability, the possibility of finally being bourgeois, civilized, and respectable.

I was the uncivilized thing in Bobby's life, reminding her of the taste of hunger, the remembered stink of her mother's sweat, her own desire. I became sex for her. I held it in me, in the push of my thighs against hers when she finally grabbed me and dragged me off into the citadel of her bedroom. I held myself up, back and off her. I did what I had to do to get her, to get myself what we both wanted. But what a price we paid for what I did.

What I did.
What I was.
What I do.
What I am.

I paid a high price to become who I am. Her contempt, her terror, were the least of it. My contempt, my terror, took over my life, because they were the first things I felt when I looked at myself, until I became unable to see my true self at all. "You're an animal," she used to say to me, in the dark with her teeth against my thigh, and I believed her, growled back at her, and swallowed all the poison she could pour into my soul.

Now I sit and think about Bobby's thighs, her legs opening in the dark where no one could see, certainly not herself. My own legs opening. That was so long ago and far away, but not so far as she finally ran when she could not stand it anymore, when the lust I made her feel got too wild, too uncivilized, too dangerous. Now I think about what I did.

What I did.
What I was.
What I do.
What I am.

"Sex." I told her. "I will be sex for you."

Never asked, "You. What will you be for me?"

Now I make sure to ask. I keep Bobby in mind when I stare at women's thighs. I finger my seams, flash my teeth, and put it right out there.

"You. What will you let yourself be for me?"

THE MUSCLES OF THE MIND

I slept through one whole year of my life—the year I did not have the money to go to graduate school the way I had expected. Being awake would have meant making decisions, and I did not know what to decide. I did not know who I was supposed to be. I dreamed through that year, heavy-lidded and silent, though I went almost every day to work as a salad girl, pickle chopper, housekeeper, waitress, substitute teacher, counter girl, or line worker in a mop factory. I could do any of that again easily—make change with one hand while wiping terrazzo with another, keep grammar school children at their desks, slice lettuce or pickles bracing the blade with the flat of my palm, rack up two hundred mops in an hour, or scrub babyshit off crib slats—but I've lost the ability to sleep during the day. I wake at first light, even if I have blacked out every window in the room, no matter how late I got to bed the night before. It is as if I had slept myself out, used up that talent in that long terrible dragged-out year, and now I'm doomed to come awake early every morning, suddenly, completely, my heart pounding in my ears as if someone were screaming in the next room.

"It's your circadian rhythm," Anna told me. "I read about it someplace—all about crickets singing at twilight even if you try to fool them into thinking it's still daytime. You—you're always gonna know when it's dawn—a useful thing when you think about it."

"Uh huh." I rubbed tired swollen eyes. "Well, tell me, do crickets ever sing at noon or nap when they feel like it?"

"Don't know." Anna gave me one of her lopsided grins. "Don't know shit about crickets, really. It's twilight I know about—that's when I wake up. Just about the time you need a little nap or something, right?"

"Something."

"Well, we an't never gonna get in phase, are we? I'm always gonna be pissed at you stumbling around making noise early in the morning, and you an't never gonna forgive me for banging pots when I get the urge to bake 'long about three in the morning. Right?"

"Probably."

Anna grinned wider still and used her elbow to wipe sweat off her eyebrows. The late afternoon sun was pouring in her big shaded windows, laying a pattern of silhouetted walnut leaves on her bare feet where they were folded up against her thighs. She was naked except for the polished white handkerchief she had spread over her lap to catch any stray grains of grass from the loose bag she was slowly pushing through her flour sifter. Like my mama, Anna believed you never washed a flour sifter, you brushed it clean. When she cleaned her grass there was a slight dusting of flour sprinkled among the pungent leaves in her mixing bowl. I didn't really smoke any more myself, but I'd tasted Anna's blend once or twice and imagined a slight baking powder aftertaste that reminded me of home. The aura of biscuits and marijuana-induced relaxation that surrounded Anna was one of the things I liked about sharing the apartment with her. She kept it calm, dimly lit, and sweet smelling.

"I'm just an old dyke hippie," she'd insisted, when I'd come to ask about the apartment.

I'd laughed, "Well, we should get along just fine then. I'm kind of a young one."

Anna had pulled her sandal strap up and then looked me up and down, from my long shaggy hair and labrys earrings to the backpack I wore over one shoulder, from the Crazy Ladies T-shirt under my army surplus jacket to my steel-toed hiking boots. She'd pushed back her short-cropped frosty grey hair, pursed her lips, and then given that grin I would learn to love.

"Kind of, maybe," she'd laughed. "You another one of these Women's Center lesbians?"

"No, I'm new in town."

"Look to me like you're new in the world, but come have a cup of tea and tell me why you'd like to live in this messy old house. I'm warning you, it's full of really crazy women, all of 'em running through here all the time trying to get me to go to one meeting or another, some demonstration or discussion group. I don't go to meetings, you understand. Three other apartments in this building, and if you're planning on holding meetings in your bedroom, you better see if you can't rent in one of them. This is the de-politicized zone in here. I bake a lot, smoke a lot, and sleep during the day, and I intend to keep it that way."

She led me in past the screened porch to a spacious living room that had an old brocade couch pushed up under the windows and a rug that was worn through in a path from the kitchen to the open bathroom door. There were lots of plants drooping in the heat, dust and cat fur clinging to the bottom of the pots. An enormous dirty white cat was sleeping in a patch of sunlight on one of the pews. Anna dropped down on a big stuffed cushion and watched me perch awkwardly on the near couch.

"Where you from?" she asked suddenly, and without thinking about it I answered, "South Carolina."

"Yeah? You got a strange accent."

"Rhode Island, spent some time there when I was a kid and my mama got sick. My family just about disowned me when I come home talking like a Yankee."

"I been to Rhode Island once. Weird place, but all North is weird to me. They talk too fast and ask too many questions." She lit a cigarette. A big black and grey tomcat walked over and plopped in her lap. She began to stroke him without looking down.

"Cats O.K., huh?"

"Mine are. They've driven off everybody else's in the building. Even old Ghostdance there wakes up when a strange cat comes a-round, eats them up, and runs them off." She looked pleased at the thought. "Us sleepy-looking types are dangerous when threatened, you know."

"Oh, I know. I been messed with myself a time or two." I dropped my bag and pulled out the stack of her apartment ads I'd torn off the bulletin board over at the Women's Center. I handed them to her and gave her my own slow grin. "I got no problem with going next door if I want to talk politics and I don't cook much anymore, so the kitchen is yours to keep. I don't smoke. I do karate, and I like to play pool, though I'm not much good at it. I work days up the street at the camera store, and I want this apartment real bad."

She grinned and shook her head. "You take down all my ads?"

"Think so, all I saw anyway. I asked around about you. Sounds like you and I could get along, and I got to move before the week's up."

She shook her head again and laughed out loud. "You picked up more than an accent in Rhode Island, picked up a few Yankee ways, didn't you?"

"No more than I need to get by." I dropped my head, looked up at her from under my eyelids, giving her my country-honey drawl. "Shit, mama, I'm just a good old girl, don't want no trouble a'tall. Easy to get along with, easy to get for that matter, and peaceable by nature."

"Uh huh."

"Uh huh," I repeated back to her.

Just like that, we were friends. Anna treated me like an ambassador from a foreign nation. Baby-dyke-politicos, she named us, after I started going to all the meetings at the Women's Center. I was twenty-four and had been dating women for more than seven years, long enough to resent being labeled a baby dyke, but Anna had been out for almost twenty years and joked that she'd had her first orgasm while wearing her Girl Scout uniform. I liked her better than any other women in the building, liked her slow, stoned drawl, her sharp, witty glances, and her invariably good-natured acid remarks when people started talking about the "women's revolution." Most of all I liked her stories. She'd been going to Panama City where there was a real gay bar with a drag show since she'd come to Tallahassee as a freshman in 1963. There wasn't a dyke in town she didn't know and no legendary piece of gossip she hadn't already heard, or been the subject of. Ten years ago, she'd been arrested with two dozen others out in front of the blackened ruins of the town's short-lived gay bar. All their names had been printed in the paper, and she'd lost her teaching fellowship in the English department.

"That was enough politics for me. I've had the longest graduate school career in history as a result. You know this is the first year they've let me teach again?" She offered me a brownie with one hand, a joint with the other. "And still, every time somebody opens a gay bar in this town, some local firebombs it. It's got to where it's easier around here for a faggot to get a liquor license than fire insurance."

"There's that pool hall over on College."

"Yeah, after one o'clock in the morning, and then only if you're real discreet, and real careful, and real young. I an't none of that, and I prefer Panama City myself. Course, you probably like those sweaty girls in tanktops that go in there and pose under those sling lamps, sneaking whiskey in their soda bottles when it an't their turn to play."

"You *have* been there."

"Hell, I've been everywhere in this town. I could tell you stories would keep you awake nights. Like the name of the boy who firebombed the last two gay bars, and exactly what year his daddy got appointed sheriff."

"Damn!" I shook my head.

"Uh huh. Course you got a few stories yourself. Don't play pool worth a damn, do you? But you bring 'em home, those sweaty girls?"

"Bar dykes." I said it flatly. "You know how it is. They got those stringy muscles in their arms, and they all grin like those old pictures of Elvis Presley getting ready to shake his butt where the camera can't see. Gets to me every time."

She laughed at me, but then put her hand on my arm in apology. "I don't know. You're younger, maybe it's different for you. Women my age now, we've always been kind of hard on each other for that kind of thing. You're supposed to do it because you're in love. You get a reputation for sleeping around and people treat you bad, call you terrible names. I always hated that, but not enough to do anything myself. To tell you the truth, the only time I ever brought anybody home that way, I was drunk and I hated it. Must be different if you're younger, huh?"

"No, not that I've seen, and the trouble is I like them older than me anyway," I'd shrugged, "older than you. And yeah, they got a word for me, too."

"I don't want to hear it."

"Neither do I." I ran my palms up my own stringy arms and looked up at the pictures she had pinned all over her bedroom door. The women up there looked back at me with pinpoint black sleepy eyes— lesbians Anna's age and older, mysterious, powerful and mean, no doubt, if you didn't play by their rules. I hugged myself and looked away. "Neither do I."

At the concert last week, I kept walking back to Cass and the little bottle of Jack Daniels she had in her coat pocket. "Have a drink, darling. It'll open your eyes," she'd say, her pupils hidden behind half-closed lids. I shook my head no and gave her a quick lick on the neck that made her cheeks flash pink and her eyes open wide. All the women near us, most of them Cass's friends from work or the pool hall, had their own bottles. I tried to get Cass to keep her little bottle down in the shadows. The crowd kept pushing past, their eyes hooded with too much dope and skin sour with cigarettes—women in party clothes: loose trousers, velvet vests, hats, high-heeled boots, glittering necklaces, and elaborate hoops dangling from their ears. Most of them looked like they belonged to the same gypsy troupe, their tribe indicated by the slogan-bearing buttons pinned to their collars and jackets. I saw Anna go by with her new girlfriend, Gayle, and then three of the women from the house—Judy, Paula, and Lenore. But none of them seemed to have seen us, and they all quickly disappeared into the audience. I felt Cass slip her hands around my waist and turned my face into the shelter of her neck.

"Where do they all come from?" I was only half-serious. There were more women in the audience than I'd seen at any demonstration up at the Capitol building.

"Oh, these only come out for the music," Cass laughed. "Just like me."

"You know, culture, women's culture." Cass's friend, Billy, leaned over us, her hand sliding past my butt on its way to the bottle in Cass's pocket. "An't you heard about women's culture?" I looked down at the black ink tattoos standing out all over her forearms. Billy was wearing her usual uniform—jeans so old and worn they looked like grey sky over the ocean at dawn, and a denim vest buttoned up tight to flatten her breasts. Her arms were bare, and every time she stretched her hand out, I could see white flash under her armpit from skin that was never exposed to the sun.

"You mean to tell me we an't here to listen to rock-and-roll?" Cass slapped Billy's shoulder and giggled. It had taken two weeks of teasing and arguing before Cass had agreed to come to this event, and she'd insisted on getting Billy and her girlfriend Roxanne to come, too. "Got to have somebody to talk to," she'd insisted.

Billy had thought the whole notion a hoot. "They don't know how to dress," she kept saying, "but some of these chicks an't bad looking."

Roxanne just kept biting the lipstick off her lips and kicking her heels against the wall behind us. "I don't see nothing here anybody'd want to take home with 'em." She lit a cigarette and gave me a look of pure malevolence. I wondered if she had seen Billy's hand on my ass. I leaned back into Cass's embrace and tried to look happily innocent of any interest in Roxanne's woman. That wasn't too hard. Cass was just about the sexiest woman in the crowd, big and rough-looking in her worn denim jacket with her black hair cut close around her ears, but with soft brown eyes and a quick smile. She was a good-natured woman who liked me more than she was sure she wanted to. More importantly, she didn't seem to feel the need that Billy did to push her girlfriends around. I loved having a woman in my life who prowled like a big old tiger, yet cuddled me close like a kitten licking mama's ears. Billy talked about Roxanne as if the woman was a not-quite-bright child, and clearly had decided I had to have some special hidden sexual talent if Cass was so ready to put up with my sass. Part of what kept me seeing Cass was her casual acceptance of my temper and habits, and her grinning dismissal of Billy's half-serious flirting with me. Cass was also nearly as tall as Billy and had told me frankly that they had become friends only after everybody they knew kept pushing them to fight each other.

"We was supposed to do the fight of the week or something, and let everybody know who was butcher than who, you know. But providing that kind of free entertainment just an't my style. Billy and I put them all through some changes when we took up with each other, I'll tell you."

Two women I had met at the Women's Center wiggled past us. One of them looked me in the eye and then up over my head into Cass's face. I could feel Cass's grin in the way her hands wiggled on me. The woman looked away quickly.

"Did you hear about Angie?" her friend asked.

"Yeah, I heard." The woman pushed away from us hurriedly. "Don't talk about her here."

"Did you see her face?" Roxanne spoke with her cigarette held between her teeth. "That woman needs to reconsider going without make-up."

I felt the heat come up in my face and didn't know for a moment if I was angry or ashamed. I watched the expressions on the faces of the women who filed past us, then felt the skin at the back of my neck pull tight. We could have been animals in a cage from the way they looked at us. I kept going from indignant anger to shame with no pause between. The anger felt healthy but wouldn't stay with me, while the shame was continuous and crippling. I wanted to be proud of Cass's hands on my hips, to glare back coldly at the women who frowned at her. I was proud of her, but my pride wasn't holding any better than my anger. I wished I didn't care what anybody thought, but I did. Beside me Roxanne kept getting her mirror out and pulling a few curls forward down over her eyes. Her hands were shaking, her make-up streaking on her neck where sweat was trailing down. For a moment, she looked like my little sister looking up at me, wanting my help but unable to ask. I could have cried. Instead, I took deep breaths trying to calm myself and finally just gave it up and took a couple of pulls from Cass's bottle.

Cass hugged me again, her eyes watching me closely. "We can always leave." She didn't look as if the idea bothered her at all.

"The music hasn't even started." I drank again, concentrating on feeling angry rather than self-conscious or ashamed. The last of the audience was milling past us while a piano chord sounded from the front of the hall. A little group of men and women passed us, the women defiant in silky skirts and the men holding the women close to them. One of the women stared at Billy and giggled when Billy grinned at her. The man with her looked nervous and impatient, but the woman didn't seem to want to head for her seat. Like a pigeon transfixed by a snake, she was pinned to the far wall by Billy's green-eyed stare. I almost laughed out loud.

"I don't care who they sleep with," I whispered to Cass, "I just wish they wouldn't tell so many lies about it."

"Mean bitch," Cass quipped, not meaning it at all.

Roxanne looked over at me strangely, her face working as if she were making up her mind about something. She looked up at Billy who was still watching the woman against the far wall. "Hell," Roxanne said, "these days I can't tell who's lying and who is just passing time."

"Passing time," I repeated. I ignored Cass's offer of another drink. Instead I turned and put my arm around Roxanne's shoulder, watching with her as the audience settled down and Cass and Billy whispered behind us. I watched the way the women moved, the muscles that stood out in their necks, the way their eyes went from dark to light in the changing light. My teeth clenched, but I just held on to Roxanne, and kept my hip pressed close to Cass's long legs.

Most mornings when I woke there in the early dawn, I would lie still and think about the stories Anna told me. She didn't really talk much to the other women in the house, not even the ones who came to sit on her waterbed and smoke her dope—none of them knew she was arrested ten years ago. "Hell, they'd put me on posters and platforms if they did." She laughed softly at the stories they told her, telling about her childhood now and then, but mostly getting them to talk. When I joined them to sit on the floor and drink a beer, Anna started teasing me about whether I'd been over playing pool.

"Just to watch," I told her, and we both laughed.

"I hate that pool hall." Mona was embroidering a red and gold labrys on the back of her jacket. She bit off red yarn and spit it into her palm. "All those drunken punks out on the sidewalk all the time, pushing those big motorbikes around, and the women in there hanging on them. Makes me sick."

"They don't all hang on the men, you know." Lenore didn't even look in my direction. "Twenty tables in there and never less than five of them have women playing each other—some pretty tough-looking women. The men stay out of their way, and that's nice to see."

"If you ask me there's no difference between those women and the men in there anyway." Judy took the bowl of sunflower seeds out of her lap and pushed it at Mona. Her face was twisted in disgust. "There's always a couple of them punching each other in the arm, arms all ugly with ink tattoos, and their girlfriends in tight skirts sitting up on stools behind them, not daring to say a word. That's what people think we are when we say we're dykes, and that's not what we are at all."

"I like tattoos," I said, "and I like women who can really play pool, play it well enough to make all those men bite their tongues. They play for money, you know. Some of them pay their way out of what they earn off those boys, and I like that, too."

"Well, I don't like it." Judy looked like she was going to spit. "Competition games, swinging those sticks like they were holding swords, carrying knives—they do you know—it's a cesspit of violence in there, and they all get off on it. People are always getting beaten up in that parking lot and women get hassled on the sidewalk all the time. I think it should be closed down."

"I think it must be different for you, all of you," Anna said after a while, carefully not looking in my direction. "When I was your age, places like that were the only way you could find other lesbians. I used to go in there and nod at women I would see nowhere else. There's a lot of women work down in the paper mills come all the way up here to sit on those stools and watch other women play pool."

"Exactly." I took another deep breath, trying not to get too angry. "You're always talking about class, Judy, the working classes supposed to make the revolution. They're the ones over there in that parking lot, leaning on tailgates, holding their own meetings."

"It's not the same thing."

"But maybe we ought to go over there and pass out leaflets some time, invite those women to a dance or something." Mona put her embroidery down. Her face was flushed and excited. Anna looked uncomfortable. Judy stared directly at me, and I could feel my neck getting hot. I wanted to say something, but I couldn't think what.

Lenore cleared her throat and cracked a few sunflower seeds. "I don't know," she giggled, "don't really feel like playing feminist evangelist to the pool hall set myself."

Anna giggled with her, and then there was a wave of laughter.

I smiled but didn't laugh. After a little while Mona started explaining just what she meant at the last consciousness-raising session at the Women's Center when she told Sharma she was antimonogamous. Someone else began to describe the sit-in at the student council that got us the funds for the rape crisis phone line. Then Mona tried to talk Anna into coming to a poetry reading the next weekend. Judy started going on and on about the article she had just read that explained why a women's revolution was inevitable at this point in history.

I sat quietly, sipping at my beer. I was exhausted from typing up the budget requests for the Day Care Center, and my stomach ached, but I didn't want to go off to bed yet. If I did, I was pretty sure I would become the next topic of conversation. Worse, I was feeling the same way I did at the concert. Part of me wanted to disappear, to become just another version of Mona or Lenore, just like everyone else.

Cass wanted to take me to the stock car races the next night, and I still didn't know if I wanted to go. I used to go to the races with my mama when I was a teenager, rooting for Bobby Allison and Fireball Roberts, eating boiled peanuts and pissing into an open trough behind the bleachers, but I hadn't done anything like that since I left home—never told anyone about it at all.

"You'll love it," Cass insisted. "Fast cars and lots of noise, and we can pinch and kiss each other when everybody jumps up to look at the crashes."

I watched Judy's face, the slim fingers that kept coming up to push her bangs over behind one ear, the white collar of her blouse startling against her tanned skin. Her eyes tracked past me when she turned her head, not stopping to risk catching my glance. I don't like her, I thought, and it surprised me to realize that. We slept together once, when I had just moved in. It had been an awkward night. She'd made a point of stopping me when I'd slid down her body, telling me she really didn't like oral sex, and she'd shrieked when I'd pushed one finger between her labia.

"Don't do that," she whispered, pulling up and planting her pubic mound firmly against my hip. What she wanted to do was climb on top of me and rock against me until she'd made herself come.

"Tribadism," I'd named it, trying to position myself so that I could enjoy it as much as she did. I really wanted to taste her, to put my tongue between her thighs, into her armpits, under her chin and behind her ears. Her hipbone hurt me and she kept lifting her torso so that I couldn't even feel the lush heat of her full breasts. I wrestled for a while, licking her salty neck, wanting to bite her and imagining that she was enjoying my tongue.

"Christ! You're making me sticky," Judy complained. She never stopping talking even while she was grinding her labia into my hipbone. "...I'm going to Gainesville on Wednesday...Oh!...want to talk to Jackie about going with me...oh...you too maybe...oh...oh...horses...want to go riding...want to go riding with me...I love to ride...Oh!"

It made me crazy, as if sex were a set of calisthenics one did to trigger sleep. When she came, she went rigid and silent, her body rising up and off of me stiffly, her eyes unfocused. I wondered what she thought then, but didn't ask. When she came back to herself, she rolled over as if it were now my turn to climb on top and do the same. I pretended to fall asleep instead just to get her to be quiet, to lie still beside me while I rested my hands on the soft swell of her hips and watched the street light flicker as the wind blew the leaves around on the trees outside. She was a lawyer's daughter from Miami and not a bad person. Not a bad person at all, I told myself, just different from me, very different from me.

It wasn't until I watched her sitting on Anna's bed, waving the smoke out of her face and going on and on, that I realized I had been mad at Judy, was still mad at her, and that actually she was probably mad at me. I hadn't really spoken much to her since we'd climbed out of bed that next morning. Watching her talking, not letting anyone say more than a sentence or two before starting to talk again, I realized her manners were like her lovemaking—imperious, self-centered, and oblivious. I preferred the women I brought home from the pool hall, the ones who liked me biting them, liked biting me, liked whispering dirty words, wrestling, and shoving their calloused fingers between my labia until I bit them harder and harder, my mouth full of the taste of them, the texture of their skin, their smoky, powerful smell, soaking them up, swallowing and swallowing. Making love with them I rise right up out of myself. I'm happy then in a way I never seem to be otherwise, sure of myself and not afraid. I lose all my self-consciousness, my fear of saying or doing the wrong thing. Their strength becomes my strength, and I love them for it. I hate the men who hassle me on the sidewalk outside the pool hall, the scary threats and the all-too-serious screams in the parking lot, but I love the hall itself, the women in there, the way they make me feel when they stand in that yellow light and rub their fingers together, looking me up and down.

In CR, one after the other, everyone insisted they did not fantasize. I looked over at Lenore guiltily, afraid to risk saying anything. There are days I am not here at all. Two cups of coffee and I run away in my mind to eerie dreams of lovemaking, the dance, the swirling turn of bodies catching the slow glint of firelight. In the mountain clearing with the women's army, I give up hatred in the arms of a demon who knows no rhetoric. If I turn my head I can see her, the Black Queen, the one with the knives, razor blade under her tongue, and a smile like the one on Cass's face as she lifts her stick to clean out some redneck boy thinks he's as fast as she is. The gloves on her hands are spiked. She teaches me to use them. She uses them on me, makes tattoos up my thighs for anyone to read. Under my clothes always, the feel of her hands on me, where no one can see. Men and women, women and men, the unguarded, the unsuspecting. Is she a man? Am I a woman?

I do not *have fantasies*. Fantasy opens me up; I become fantasy. I am the dangerous daughter, thigh-stroking, soft-tongued lover, the pit, the well, the well of horniness, laughter rolling up out of me like gravy boiling over the edge of a pan. I become the romantic, the mystic, the one without shame, rocking myself on the hip of a rock, a woman as sharp as coral. I make in my mind the muscle that endures, tame rage and hunger to spirit and blood. I become the rock. I become the knife. I am myself the mystery. The me that will be waits for me. If I cannot dream myself new, how will I find my true self?

"What about you?" Judy leaned toward me with an intent expression. "Do you have fantasies?"

The roar in my ears was my heart, an ocean of shame and rage. My leg muscles pulled tight and cramp. My belly turned liquid and hot under my navel. I would throw up if I opened my mouth. I would throw up. My muscles failed me, failed me completely.

"Not much, not really." Peter denied Christ three times before cockcrow. I cursed myself for being such a piece of shit, such a piece of chickenshit. "Not any more, not really." I kept my eyes on my hands where they twisted in my lap. If I looked up I might say anything, anything.

Waking up and not being able to go back to sleep, I sit with a cup of coffee and my journal. I've kept one off and on since school, after the guidance counselor told me it was a way to keep control of your life, to look back and see your own changes. I don't look back at it much though, never seem to have the time, but it doesn't matter. Sometimes writing in it is a way of smoothing things out inside me. The morning after the concert, I didn't write about the concert or Roxanne or even Cass. I wrote about the muscles of the mind, what my old *sensei* used to call the secret of all karate, the disciplined belief in yourself.

"We are under so many illusions about our powers," I wrote, "illusions that vary with the moon, the mood, the moment. Waxing, we are all-powerful. We are the mother-destroyers, She-Who-Eats-Her-Young, devours her lover, her own heart; great-winged midnight creatures and the witches of legend. Waning, we are powerless. We are the outlaws of the earth, daughters of nightmare, victimized, raped, and abandoned in our own bodies. We tell ourselves lies and pretend not to know the difference. It takes all we have to know the truth, to believe in ourselves without reference to moon or magic.

"The only magic we have is what we make in ourselves, the muscles we build up on the inside, the sense of belief we create from nothing. I used to watch my mama hold off terror with only the edges of her own eyes for a shield, and I still don't know how she did it. But I am her daughter and have as much muscle in me as she ever did. It's just that some days I am not strong enough. I stretch myself out a little, and then my own fear pulls me back in. The shaking starts inside. Then I have to stretch myself again. Waxing and waning through my life, maybe I'm building up layers of strength inside. Maybe."

Last night, late, Liz called, asked me to please go out with her for a beer—meet her at the Overpass and talk to her for a few hours. She needed someone to listen to her. Jackie never did anymore, she said. But when we sat down she acted like a stranger, like someone who had come in from out of town and really couldn't stay long. She was smoking again, Pall Malls out of a hard pack, and lighting them with wooden kitchen matches from a small box. Her red hair looked faded, its dark shine had gone dull and even the blue of her eyes had faded to grey.

"It's wearing me down," she kept saying. "It's just fucking wearing me down."

I ordered her a beer and me a glass of wine. When she kept licking her lips and lighting cigarettes one after the other, I started telling her stories. I found myself describing Judy's hip-grinding routine and the way my new girlfriend Cass would spit in her hand and slide her pool cue up and down while other women took their shots—making both acts equally hilarious and revealing.

"Bitches," Liz pronounced them both.

"Like you and me, honey. We're all pretty bitchy when it comes down to it." I rubbed my hands in the wine that had trailed down the lip of my glass.

"Naw." She'd downed her beer and signaled for another one. "You and me, we're the ones they fuck with. We're something else, taking their shit all the time, their goddamn shit all the time."

I'd sipped my wine and rubbed my neck. "You and Jackie fighting then?"

"How'd you guess?" In the dim bar's lighting, her pale eyes looked charcoal, and she had no smile at all. She was wearing the collar of her dark plaid shirt turned up high against the fringe of her short cropped hair and she kept pushing up at the back of her head until the hair was standing up stiff and spiky. She looked like one of those desperate women sketched out on the cover of an old Ann Bannon novel, lips and eyes swollen and dark, features all raw and flushed.

"I should have known better, I really should have, you know?" She poured beer down her throat with a quick dramatic gesture, a Bette Davis move from a great thirties movie. So quick and sudden she moved, it seemed as if the beer never even touched her tongue, as if her thirst were all for the feel of it hitting her stomach, and not to ease the bitterness in her mouth.

"I an't no kid. I got two kids of my own after all. And hell, I went through all this with Richard, thinking that we were different, that we were special." There were tears in her eyes, I saw, waiting there, not falling but shining. She kept moving her head, shaking her hair and pushing it up again. "Only special thing in the world is the lies we tell ourselves, make ourselves believe. Stupid, stupid bitches always thinking this time it's different."

Too much for me, I thought, sighed and tilted my glass to match the speed with which she threw back hers. I drank with her one for one, until dizziness made my hands loose on the glass, and I knew I had to slow it down. Liz didn't seem to notice. Her eyes were turned in on herself and her sudden laughs never altered her expression. Liz knew things about me no one else did, and because of that had a right to call me up in the night and ask for help. We had never been lovers, but we had always been friends. She had known me when I was in college, when I was the only lesbian she'd ever met. She had given me enough help when I had needed it, even cleaned me up and asked no questions one night when I showed up on her doorstep, my nose running blood and my clothes all torn. I had introduced her to Jackie and helped her move when she decided to leave her husband, but I couldn't think of what to say to her now.

"Everybody fights, lovers more than anyone else," I tried to tell her. "It's part of wanting so much from each other. Sometimes you crawl all over each other's nerves without intending to. . . ." She didn't seem to hear me. She was watching the men around us and not looking at me at all.

"Richard says if I come back, we'll move out to the land co-op and have our own house up by next spring," she said finally. The wine in my mouth went sour with the thought of Richard, with his smug little smile and those copies of the *Militant* he always had tucked under one arm. The man was fatuous and self-congratulatory in a way that ate at my insides, going on and on about the laboring classes while living off the income of an apartment building his daddy had turned over to him after graduation.

"Pond scum," I'd called him once, a line Jackie had repeated to him with great relish. I stared at the foam in Liz's glass as it went flat. I couldn't think of anything to say to her about Richard.

"I could put in a garden out there," Liz told me, keeping her eyes on her glass, "be with Mikey and Janine all the time, not have to go back to that damn office every damned day."

I'd thumped my glass against hers, forcing her to look up at me. "Yeah, and Richard could tell all his buddies how patience had been the secret—you know that line—how all he had to do was wait for you to get it out of your system. You and Jackie. . ."

"JACKIE!" Her wet glass slapped the table. "Hell, I never even see her anymore. She's always at work, or the Women's Center, or I'm at work, or Mikey's sick, or Janine's crying and Jackie has to go off for a walk to clear her head, or Jackie's goddamned aunt is there going on about how hard she used to work. . . ." Liz stopped, wiped her eyes and her mouth and then looked directly into my face. "It's not what I wanted, not anything near what I thought it would be. It's just not."

"It's no worse than anybody else has."

"It's worse. It's me." She looked sideways at the men at the bar. "If I was living out at the co-op, Jackie and I could still see each other now and then. Richard wouldn't have to know, and I wouldn't be so tired, so damned tired all the time. You know, you know how it is, I hate being poor. I never intended to be poor again, and Christ! We're just above starving." Her face was too fierce for argument. The wine rose up in my throat, bitter and embarrassing. I didn't know what to say. I just didn't know what to say.

Waking up at dawn, I push myself out of bed, head for the bathroom, piss, rinse my mouth, and pull on shorts and a sweatshirt. It's seven steps down to the sidewalk from the side porch, and I take them at a run, pushing myself to get the momentum for running all the way up the hill to the campus. My head pounds and my throat hurts, and I have to grit my teeth to make myself run. I hate waking up after drinking wine, with that sick taste in my mouth. Cass says that wine is worse than whiskey, that it stays in your body longer and is harder on your kidneys. Cass talks a lot about her kidneys. She rolled her truck a few years ago—*bounced off that steering wheel, till I wished I'd of died*—and did herself some serious damage. Her kidneys are the worst of it, so that sometimes when she leans over to take a shot at the pool hall, her face will screw up and she'll stand back quickly, and curse.

"Hurts like a motherfucker," she says. But she won't stop drinking. "Got to drink to ease the pain," she laughs. I don't argue with her, not about her drinking anyway. We got enough to argue about without that.

"You been seeing Cass a while," Anna said to me the other night.

"Must be time she got fed up with me, then." I kept my face turned away, picked up Ghostdance and hugged her to my neck.

"Well, if you going to go on the way you been, I expect it is." Anna's voice was low and sad. I watched her eyes track over to the pictures on her wall—old lovers and lost friends, she'd called it one night—her wall of grief. "I expect it is."

On the hill above the science building, the dogwood trees are in bloom. My legs shake when I stop and bend over. I hold my balance and stretch out slowly, feeling the sweat running down my back. My thighs tremble and my throat still aches. When I look over at the Science Building's huge mirrored front, I can see myself reflected in the glass, my hair swinging in the sunlight, the wet grass shining under my shoes. I look tiny and hard, like a nail sticking up out of the ground.

"*Ten-no-kata-sho*," I say out loud, and face punch up into my reflected image. The adrenalin comes even though all I have to trigger it is my own frustration. The *sensei* at the school I've been going to these past few months is a returned vet and a part-time cop who keeps switching back and forth, talking now in fortune-cookie confucianism and then with macho insistence. Once every few weeks he loses control and really pops one of the boys. He doesn't know how to deal with the women at all, and we all know he'd be happier if we weren't in the class. The six of us who have remained ignore everything except the skills he has to teach us. For all of us, it is the discipline that matters, making ourselves over into what we most want to be, becoming strong for ourselves. We strip off our sex with our jewelry, sometimes so thoroughly that he forgets to treat us like the fragile incompetents he believes us to be. Last week he lost patience with me the way he does with the boys, grabbed me by the arm and shook me.

"You're behaving like a passenger here, going through the motions. You're not thinking about what you're doing. You're not in control. Come on. Get into your body. Feel it, feel what you're doing. Push those muscles, feel 'em."

"The muscles of the mind," I'd thought, "I'm just a passenger in here. I got to do something about the muscles of the mind."

I watch myself in the wall of glass above me, watch my back as I turn and lift my arms. I make my trembling muscles coil and reach, hoping desperately that the magic will come, that the *kata* will become sex for me the way it sometimes does. I slip into stance, determinedly loose, trying to thoughtlessly snap out the tension, to turn and jerk crisply, sharply, my shadow under me a pinpoint like the light in the pupils of Liz's eyes. I push and sweat, but my mind won't let go. My feet keep slipping in the grass. The sun slanting up through the dogwood trees stabs my eyes. I lose my place in the *kata* and can't remember the next sequence of moves.

"Goddamn it!" I shout, and my voice echoes back to me off the building. I see myself again, my mouth open like any screaming woman, the dizzy image of window after window reflecting figure after figure. I watch myself, the way I saw myself last night in the bathroom at the Overpass, reflected in the ammonia-stained tiles, my wrists coming up to face-punch the mirror. The morning sunlight was brighter than the fluorescent lights in the bathroom had been. I had been wavery and indistinct in the tiles. Now I was crisp and sharp in the mirrored windows. There were dozens of me up there, all open-mouthed and sunlit, bleached nails in the ground, not rising up, being hammered down. I lean over, seeing myself lean over, and remem-

ber Roxanne at the concert, the way she kept dropping her head so
her hair fell across her face, the same posture I have in every picture
I've got from high school.

"Maybe you an't so bad," Roxanne had told me when we'd gone
off to the bathroom together at the concert. "But you really ought
to think about using a little make-up. Cass is known for taking up
with good-looking women—women who know how to present themselves, you know?" I'd just nodded and said nothing. I could touch
Roxanne's shoulder, share a sip of whiskey with her, but I didn't know
how to begin to talk to her, how to say I wasn't looking to hold on
to Cass the way she wanted to cling to Billy. But then I hadn't known
how to talk to Liz last night either, to tell her what to do. I don't
want to be poor myself. At bottom maybe it's all about what you
can stand and what you can't. Certainly I wouldn't be able to stand
living with Richard any more than I could Billy, but I can imagine
things that might help Liz—starting with a decent income, day care
for Mikey and Janine, work that wouldn't leave her exhausted and
crazy—all the things none of us can give her. What would help Billy
and Cass, or Roxanne, or even me?

I stretch up again, start the *kata* over, watching my form in the
mirrored windows, the pattern of my body twisting, rising, kicking,
and coming back around to start again. I start again, finish the form,
and start a third time. Sweat runs into my eyes, and my muscles go
loose and fluid. The magic starts in my belly, and the *kata* becomes
smooth, the feel of it more like sex than anything else. My fear goes
out of me, my grief. What did I imagine was wrong with me anyway?
The first night I'd slept with Cass, I'd rolled over and laughed out
loud when we'd finished making love.

"Goddamn!" I'd yelled. "I love my life." Cass had laughed back
into my face, pulling me down to start all over again.

"Goddamn," I whisper now, and start the *kata* over a fourth time.
Liquid and gold, my knees come up and my fists punch out. The
kata, the dance, takes me up, makes me over. I let go of Liz and Judy
and all of them. I come back into stance, with my hair loose and
damp on my neck, the smell of my own body like wine in the morning sun.

"Goddamn!" I hiss the word between my teeth and look up to
see myself standing with my head back and face glowing in the reflected
windows. The whisper carries distinctly in the morning quiet. I can
almost see the ripple of it in the grass.

"Goddamn."

VIOLENCE AGAINST WOMEN BEGINS AT HOME

Paula swears that if I joined her yoga class, I would never need another chiropractor in my life. She may be right. Margaret says it's sex.

"*Everything* is about sex, but a bad back? That's the worst. It's the congestion, all that compression and tension. You know, tighter and tighter. You got to have a release, and sex is the thing that'll do it for you."

I nod and light another Marlboro. Last week, my boss finally told me they were going to have to lay me off the first of next month. I've been swinging back and forth from exhilaration to a kind of mad dread since then. God knows I hate that job, but thinking about looking for another one makes my stomach ache and my throat go dry. It makes me want to drink lots of beer and smoke endless cigarettes. What I've actually been doing is staying up late baking coffee-fudge cookies, eating them till I puke, and then going to bed to cry myself to sleep. I get to work late, barely able to sit at my keyboard. If they weren't already going to lay me off, they'd fire me.

"You haven't quit yet, huh?" Paula waves her hand as if warding off smoke, though the air conditioner over our heads has already sucked up the thin blue cloud. It's the reason I got here first and sat in just this seat—now I can just smile and not reply. I've known Paula a long time, and no response is always best with her unless you're prepared to sit still for several hours of exhaustive argument, something I haven't wanted to do since we left the feminist collective where we both used to live.

"You've got such an addictive personality. Can't you see what those cigarettes are doing to you?"

I smile determinedly and take another drag. About five years ago Paula won an award for her presentation to the therapists' collective on how fingernail biting was a form of subliminal alcoholic behavior. Since then she's become the world's expert on addictive behavior, talking on the radio and writing a pithy little column for the local women's paper. Margaret jokes that Paula can spot addiction indicators faster than most people can locate a taxi. It gets tiresome for her old friends, but most of us pretend to ignore it. Occasionally Margaret and I even talk about how tolerant we all seem to have become of each other. "It's getting older," Margaret thinks. I tell her all that has happened is that we've worn each other down. It's a conversation we have often, every time Paula or Jackie does something that gets us mad, and Margaret and I have a tacit agreement to head off arguments when we can. This time Margaret fails me.

"Paula's right," she says, pausing to lick salt off the rim of her glass. "You really ought to take a close look at yourself, girl."

"Don't want to get too introspective." I pull smoke deep into my lungs and try to look amused rather than brooding.

Margaret's eyebrows go up quizzically, and I know it's time to get to the point of this little gathering.

"I thought we were here to talk about Jackie." That sets Margaret to nodding.

"Oh Lord, don't tell me." Paula leans forward in her seat and grips her wine glass more tightly. "What's she done now?"

"It's the worst. You won't believe it." Margaret's voice is a little loud and excited. Twin spots of flush pink appear high on her cheekbones. She signals the waiter for another margarita and puts her right hand on Paula's free wrist. "She's paying the whole bill for the arbitrator. She's decided it's her own fault after all."

"Oh, that's ridiculous!"

It is that, I think, but I heard about this last night so I'm not as surprised as Paula. I let my eyes wander to the waiter's trousers drawn tight across his ass. He looks like he's put concentrated attention into that ass or else is what Bruce always calls "genetics' gift to faggots." Bruce was the first gay man I met who admitted to having grown up and come out in a poor family in a small Southern town— the same little crossroads town where I was born. Once every few months we get together to share gossip from our mothers, and talk bitchy trash that makes us both feel cosmopolitan and witty. "No one else talks like you do, honey," Bruce insists, but the truth is no one talks like either of us. Most of the other expatriate Southerners we know pretend to membership in the petty aristocracy, a fact we both find very amusing. One would think Southern gentry produced only queer offspring. Somehow the conversation always seems to turn to highly detailed descriptions of our favorite body parts. The only serious conflict Bruce and I have is our divergent fascinations. He's consumed with lust for narrow ankles and beautiful feet, while I obsess over lush behinds.

"Taste," Bruce calls it.

"Fetish," I always tell him.

I don't seem to care so much what the rest of the body is like. It's those flexing, bouncing bottoms that always pull my own thigh muscles tight and make me feel slightly gushy all over. Paula tells me I am disgustingly predictable. "A product of modern advertising, that's all you are." She's probably right. I used to be the only woman in the collective that subscribed to *Playboy*. I'd clip the pictures I liked and leave the rest of it in the trash, upsetting Paula and Jackie terribly. But I noticed that the magazine was never there when I checked back later, so one of them was probably taking it out—to verify just how sexist it was, no doubt.

"I'm not as predictable as you think," I've always told Paula, noting that she dates only bodybuilders and competition jocks. I like jocks myself, but since my taste in behinds is significantly larger than the social standard, I'm much more interested in Janet Jackson-type dancers than the tennis players Jackie and Paula go after. I can't stand skinny butts on men or women—something about them makes me nervous and uncomfortable—while a rounded, high behind, what Bruce calls a "bubble butt," always brings a flush to my neck. The waiter leans over the table next to us, and I see that he has a faint blush of pink eyeshadow under his brows and a tiny gold earring in his left ear. I am immediately entranced, and startled when Margaret grabs my wrist.

"Jackie can't deal with confrontation, you know. Never could," Margaret goes on. "It's easier for her to give in and pretend the whole thing was her fault. I'm surprised she didn't offer to pay for the spray paint they used." Margaret nods at the waiter pleasantly as he takes her empty glass, while I lean forward slightly trying to see if his other ear is pierced. Paula sees what I am doing and frowns.

"Christ, you really don't know how to behave, do you?"

"What?" Margaret has seen nothing and doesn't understand what Paula is talking about. I pass my glass to the waiter.

"Another beer," I tell him with a grin, and watch Paula's mouth tighten with rage. The waiter ignores her and smiles at me, his eyes lingering on the ancient set of figures I pulled off a charm bracelet and hung from the half dozen rings in my ears.

"I don't know what you think you're doing," Paula hisses, as he walks away.

"Flirting with a queen." I smile at her lazily. "Gonna call the Lesbian Thought Police on me? Betcha it's something Fawn and Pris could handle in an afternoon. They could come 'round with a couple of gallons of paint and a few hours to kill. No sweat."

"Are you drunk?" Paula has that righteous expression that always provoked me to rage when we were living together.

"Oh shit." I give Margaret a tired smile hoping she'll rescue me.

"Of course she's not," Margaret throws in immediately. That's Margaret's third margarita the waiter is bringing back. Lately, she and I have discussed how tiresome it is that the women's community has suddenly discovered alcoholism after all these years. There are letters to the editor in the women's papers and well-meaning workshops at every possible feminist gathering, most of which smack of self-congratulatory evangelism. Like Paula, everybody begins first by talking about how healthy they are and how pitiful the poor alcoholic is. It reminds me too much of the prayer meetings I hated so as a child. How could you ever know if you were in a state of grace or not, and why did the people who were so sure of themselves always seem to be hiding something? What I love about Margaret is that she's never sure of much of anything.

"What do you think? Do you think I'm an alcoholic?" Margaret asked me the last time we went out to dinner together. "Lee wants me to talk to my therapist about how much I drink."

I'd shrugged. "Is it getting in the way of anything you want to do?" That was a silly question, since obviously drinking is getting in the way of her and Lee living happily ever after, which is the one thing Margaret is absolutely sure she wants to do.

"Well," she'd hesitated, then shrugged, "no more than working for a living and taking care of my mother." Margaret works as the head teller at a midtown bank, a job that's a little like living on the firing line in a small arms tournament. She spends her weekends picking up after her mother, a beautiful but prematurely senile woman whose four married children have left her to Margaret to nurse and protect.

"Mama shit on that blue chintz couch again last week, and you know how embarrassing that is for her. Took me three hours to get it even half clean. I'm thinking I may have to re-cover it, but then I suppose she'll just have another accident. The doctor said I should have the furniture covered in plastic, that it's just gonna get worse, but damn, I can't do that to her. It took her so long to get some nice things, and she loves them so."

I didn't tell her what I thought, that mostly Mama didn't notice much of what she sat on anymore. It's taken Margaret years to be able to afford to buy her mother the things they both always wanted, and it would break Margaret's heart to give any of it up. Instead I'd changed the subject with a story about my mama's attempts to get flowers to grow in her swampy yard. Margaret and I both know that some time in the next year she's gonna have to give up and put her mama in a hospital of some kind. It's one of the things neither of us discusses with Paula. If Paula were to make one of her righteous comments about Margaret's mother and the wisdom of nursing homes, Margaret might do something sudden and terrible.

"I only hope you know what you're doing." Paula slaps her glass down and glares at me and Margaret.

For a moment I've lost the thread of the conversation, something I've been doing a lot lately. The fact is I have been drinking too much, and not sleeping and not eating, and half the time I can't quite keep up with what's going on around me. It's as if I wander away in my mind. Everything someone says reminds me of something someone else said, and I never get around to paying attention to the here and now. I've even gotten lost on the way to work, missed my subway stop, and taken the whole day off as a result. This time I decide to pull myself together. Paula is looking angry, and Margaret is looking confused. I shrug in Paula's direction and fish a piece of ice out of my water glass to rub across the back of my neck.

"Come on, Paula," I drop the half-melted ice back into my glass and wipe my hands on a napkin. "You lecture your friends, Margaret works too hard, Jackie lets herself be pushed around, and I flirt. It's our natures. In all the time we've known each other, none of us has changed a bit."

Paula's face freezes for a moment, then loosens, and her lips pull up slightly as if she would smile but can't quite. Instead she reaches across the table and puts her hand on mine. "We've changed. We've all changed. I can remember when you would never talk back to anybody, when Margaret was on unemployment more than she worked, and Jackie would have bounced Fawn's head off Pris's backside before she would have let them fuck with her."

She's right, but it's a shock to hear her say it. It's a shock to remember her as she used to be, the blunt and perceptive Paula who used to make me laugh all night with her caustic dissections of our neighbors. I loved her for it once, and stopped loving her when she got too careful to say those things any more. It's amazing what we have put up with from each other over the years, what we have seen each other go through, and what we have put each other through. Whenever I wonder why people hang onto old friends so desperately, I remember Jackie telling me she felt like her friends were the only record she had of what had happened in her life. "You still keep a journal?" she asked me. "I've always imagined that someday I might sit down and read all those journals you kept, see what happened that I wasn't keeping track of."

"It's Jackie we ought to be talking about. She needs our help." Margaret puts both hands back on the table and looks at Paula and me expectantly.

"What about Fawn and Pris?" I ask her. "I've got a few things to say about them."

"I think they need someone to really confront them with what they did," Paula's voice has gone flat again, her face become impassive. "That kind of thing doesn't come out of nowhere."

"Confront," I mouth back to her, wondering if all the women who use that word so easily know what they mean by it. I know what Paula's gonna say now before she says it. She's never seemed to notice how predictably her judgments peel off when she's acting like the feminist therapist, like so many layers of toasted onion, each clinging delicately to the lower layers.

"Jackie should have taken them to court," Margaret announces.

I stare at Margaret in surprise. I've been thinking the same thing for weeks. Certainly if two women had broken into my apartment and trashed it, I'd have had them in court before they'd known what was happening, but Margaret is the last one of us I'd ever expect to advocate using what she has always called "the patriarchal legal system."

"You don't mean that." Paula is as surprised as I am. The waiter slips Margaret's drink around Paula's shoulder and passes me my beer with a lazy grin. I'm tempted to grin back, but only nod. Margaret wets a forefinger and takes another taste of salt.

"I do. Arbitration isn't gonna get Jackie anywhere. Look, she didn't even get her broken glass paid for, and now she's been talked into 'accepting her responsibility' for what happened. That's crazy. She didn't do anything, and I don't think her paintings are pornographic. She's always worked on nudes, for Christ's sake! And besides, she told me she did those paintings for the study of the light and shade and the texture..."

"Oh, give me a break!" It's all I can do it keep from hissing in rage. "You know Jackie as well as I do. She's got boxes of drawings and paintings like the ones Fawn and Pris decided were so terrible. She's been doing them forever—women with knives, women with swords, in leather clothing, on motorcycles, wrestling, running naked down city streets, fucking. You've seen them. I've seen them— the ones she keeps locked up in boxes in her closet or under her bed, the ones she doesn't burn when she gets all panicky about why she does them in the first place. I just wish she'd pull them all out and plaster them over the walls of the women's bookstore, not start pretending she didn't mean to do them in the first place."

"Jackie's an artist," Paula interrupts me. "She has to work her stuff out in her own way."

"With Fawn and Pris's help she'll get it all worked out, destroy all the work she's ever done, and never do any more. Oh well, maybe they'll let her do some posters for the Take Back the Night Campaign, maybe some illustrations for the editorial page of that paper you do your column for, huh Paula? Or damn, maybe even a comic strip, if she doesn't make it too explicit..."

"You're yelling." Margaret's voice is very quiet.

I stop and look at her. Her face is pale and her fingers are curled tightly on the table. I sigh and push my beer glass forward until it clicks against Paula's wine glass. "All right. All right. What do you think we should do?" I ask her. "How do we get Fawn and Pris off her back and put her back together now that she's decided she's some kind of erotic criminal?"

"Neither Fawn nor Pris is going to do anything more to Jackie."

"Nothing justifies what they already did to Jackie's apartment. She's gonna be months replacing all her dishes." Margaret's features have the pained indignation of a woman who's had to replace her mama's glassware too often in the last year. "And to spray paint that slogan on the walls. That was the worst. *Violence against women begins at home!* That's outrageous!"

"But think about what they meant by it." Paula is trying to look patient and understanding, but sweat is starting to show on her upper lip.

I feel nauseous. "It seems to me you could make a political comment short of breaking somebody's dishes and trashing their apartment."

"Well, the thing is I've agreed to take part in the arbitration." Paula has the grace to look momentarily uncomfortable. "As an old friend of Jackie's I didn't think I should before, but Fawn and Pris have asked me, too, and I think I can get some things worked out between them all."

Margaret looks stunned. So do I probably, but my voice is calm when I speak. "You gonna get them to work out paying for Jackie's apartment?"

"That may be a problem. Neither of them has any money. Pris is only working part-time, and Fawn is still volunteering at the coffee-house while she finishes her studies. It's Jackie who has a full-time job." Paula sips her wine and looks toward the clock over the bar. She wipes her mouth with her napkin and carefully avoids my eyes. "I'm gonna be late, you know."

"Oh?" Margaret looks up to the clock on the wall and jumps in her seat. "Oh, yeah. I've got to get home too." She finishes her margarita in a gulp but doesn't move. "Look, do you think maybe we could hold a rent party for Jackie, get her some money to fix her place back up?"

Paula looks impatient and starts gathering up her stuff. "Oh, I don't think we should do that. Not while they're still in arbitration. And anyway, we have so many important things we have to raise money for this spring—community things."

"Jackie's a part of the community," I hear myself say.

"Well, of course," Paula stands up. "We all are." The look she gives me makes me wonder if she really believes that, but she's gone before I can say anything else.

"I want to do something," Margaret tells me. It looks like there are tears in her eyes. "I'm tired of not doing anything when these things happen, just talking about how horrible it all is and then going on with our lives. I want to call Jackie, or maybe even Fran and Pris."

"No, not them." I get a cold chill down my back, imagining Fran and Pris walking in on Margaret's mama some day. "That rent party idea is a good notion. I'll give Jackie a call, and you and I can set it up. It'll be like old times."

Margaret's face relaxes. She stands up, but then stops and leans across the table to kiss me on the cheek. "Old times," she laughs. "I've had some of my best times with you, you know."

"I know."

I watch Margaret walk away and shake my head. Margaret has gotten so skinny, she almost has no ass at all anymore. When I first met her she looked just like a Botticelli virgin, all lush and pink and full. I'd flirted with her for two years until she would go to bed with me, but then we'd spent the night in giggles. "Get serious," I'd kept insisting, but neither of us could. After a while we'd given up the idea of sex and just relaxed into cuddling and telling stories. Once every few years we try it again, but with the same result.

"Maybe it's how we smell to each other," Margaret once suggested. "I read about that somewhere. Or maybe we just know each other too well, huh?" I'd been laughing so hard at the time I hadn't been able to reply. I don't really care any more what it is that makes us so unsuited as lovers. We've become the best of friends. Not like Paula and I: we've been snipping at each other ever since we stopped being lovers.

I wonder if Paula still drinks half a glass of vodka to put herself to sleep every night and if she's still seeing Fawn now and then. For a moment I think about all the things we never say to each other, the things we know that we don't admit we know. Dirt. Gossip. Simple cruelty and self-righteousness.

I remember the first time Jackie showed me her drawings, the fear and uncertainty in her face, the fierceness on the features of the women she had drawn. I had liked the drawings. I had loved the passion in Jackie when she held them, the way she ground her teeth together as I lifted one after the other. I had wanted to tell her it would be all right, that people would love her warrior women, that I loved the way they threw their heads back and stared out of the drawings. Jackie seemed so fragile with her drawings spread out before her, like those white mountain flowers that come up in the spring on sturdy stalks but lose their blossoms if the wind hits them too suddenly. That's exactly what she's like, tough and wiry and sure to stand up to violence, but just as much at risk. I wonder if she has burned the drawings that Fawn and Pris didn't find.

A LESBIAN APPETITE

Biscuits. I dream about baking biscuits, sifting flour, baking powder, and salt together, measuring out shortening and buttermilk by eye, and rolling it all out with flour-dusted fingers. Beans. I dream about picking over beans, soaking them overnight, chopping pork fat, slicing onions, putting it all in a great iron pot to bubble for hour after hour until all the world smells of salt and heat and the sweat that used to pool on my mama's neck. Greens. Mustard greens, collards, turnip greens and poke—can't find them anywhere in the shops up North. In the middle of the night I wake up desperate for the taste of greens, get up and find a 24-hour deli that still has a can of spinach and half a pound of bacon. I fry the bacon, dump it in the spinach, bring the whole mess to a boil and eat it with tears in my eyes. It doesn't taste like anything I really wanted to have. When I find frozen collards in the Safeway, I buy five bags and store them away. Then all I have to do is persuade the butcher to let me have a pack of neck bones. Having those wrapped packages in the freezer reassures me almost as much as money in the bank. If I wake up with bad dreams there will at least be something I want to eat.

Red beans and rice, chicken necks and dumplings, pot roast with vinegar and cloves stuck in the onions, salmon patties with white sauce, refried beans on warm tortillas, sweet duck with scallions and pancakes, lamb cooked with olive oil and lemon slices, pan-fried pork chops and red-eye gravy, potato pancakes with applesauce, polenta with spaghetti sauce floating on top—food is more than sustenance; it is history. I remember women by what we ate together, what they dug out of the freezer after we'd made love for hours. I've only had one lover who didn't want to eat at all. We didn't last long. The sex was good, but I couldn't think what to do with her when the sex was finished. We drank spring water together and fought a lot.

I grew an ulcer in my belly once I was out in the world on my own. I think of it as an always angry place inside me, a tyranny that takes good food and turns it like a blade scraping at the hard place where I try to hide my temper. Some days I think it is the rightful reward for my childhood. If I had eaten right, Lee used to tell me, there would never have been any trouble.

"Rickets, poor eyesight, appendicitis, warts, and bad skin," she insisted, "they're all caused by bad eating habits, poor diet."

It's true. The diet of poor Southerners is among the worst in the world, though it's tasty, very tasty. There's pork fat or chicken grease in every dish, white sugar in the cobblers, pralines, and fudge, and flour, fat, and salt in the gravies—lots of salt in everything. The vegetables get cooked to limp strands with no fiber left at all. Mothers give sidemeat to their toddlers as pacifiers and slip them whiskey with honey at the first sign of teething, a cold, or a fever. Most of my cousins lost their teeth in their twenties and took up drinking as easily as they put sugar in their iced tea. I try not to eat so much sugar, try not to drink, try to limit pork and salt and white flour, but the truth is I am always hungry for it—the smell and taste of the food my mama fed me.

Poor white trash I am for sure. I eat shit food and am not worthy. My family starts with good teeth but loses them early. Five of my cousins bled to death before thirty-five, their stomachs finally surrendering to sugar and whiskey and fat and salt. I've given it up. If I cannot eat what I want, then I'll eat what I must, but my dreams will always be flooded with salt and grease, crisp fried stuff that sweetens my mouth and feeds my soul. I would rather starve death than myself.

In college it was seven cups of coffee a day after a breakfast of dry-roasted nuts and Coca-Cola. Too much grey meat and reheated potatoes led me to develop a taste for peanut butter with honey, coleslaw with raisins, and pale, sad vegetables that never disturbed anything at all. When I started throwing up before classes, my roommate fed me fat pink pills her doctor had given her. My stomach shrank to a stone in my belly. I lived on pink pills, coffee, and Dexedrine until I could go home and use hot biscuits to scoop up cold tomato soup at my mama's table. The biscuits dripped memories as well as butter: Uncle Lucius rolling in at dawn, eating a big breakfast with us all, and stealing mama's tools when he left; or Aunt Panama at the door with her six daughters, screaming, *That bastard's made me pregnant again just to get a son,* and wanting butter beans with sliced tomatoes before she would calm down. Cold chicken in a towel meant Aunt Alma was staying over, cooking her usual six birds at a time. *Raising eleven kids I never learned how to cook for less than fifteen.* Red dye stains on the sink was a sure sign Reese was dating some new boy, baking him a Red Velvet Cake my stepfather would want for himself.

"It's good to watch you eat," my mama smiled at me, around her loose teeth. "It's just so good to watch you eat." She packed up a batch of her biscuits when I got ready to leave, stuffed them with cheese and fatback. On the bus going back to school I'd hug them to my belly, using their bulk to remind me who I was.

When the government hired me to be a clerk for the Social Security Administration, I was sent to Miami Beach where they put me up in a crumbling old hotel right on the water while teaching me all the regulations. The instructors took turns taking us out to dinner. Mr. McCullum took an interest in me, told me Miami Beach had the best food in the world, bought me an order of Oysters Rockefeller one night, and medallions of veal with wine sauce the next. If he was gonna pay for it, I would eat it, but it was all like food seen on a movie screen. It had the shape and shine of luxury but tasted like nothing at all. But I fell in love with Wolfe's Cafeteria and got up early every morning to walk there and eat their danish stuffed with cream cheese and raisins.

"The best sweet biscuit in Miami," I told the counter man.

"*Nu?*" he grinned at the woman beside me, her face wrinkling up as she blushed and smiled at me.

"*Nischt,*" she laughed. I didn't understand a word but I nodded anyway. They were probably talking about food.

When I couldn't sleep, I read Franz Kafka in my hotel room, thinking about him working for the social security administration in Prague. Kafka would work late and eat polish sausage for dinner, sitting over a notebook in which he would write all night. I wrote letters like novels that I never mailed. When the chairman of the local office promised us all a real treat, I finally rebelled and refused to eat the raw clams Mr. McCullum said were "the best in the world." While everyone around me sliced lemons and slurped up pink and grey morsels, I filled myself up with little white oyster crackers and tried not to look at the lobsters waiting to die, thrashing around in their plastic tanks.

"It's good to watch you eat," Mona told me, serving me dill bread, sour cream, and fresh tomatoes. "You do it with such obvious enjoyment." She drove us up to visit her family in Georgia, talking about what a great cook her mama was. My mouth watered, and we stopped three times for boiled peanuts. I wanted to make love in the back seat of her old DeSoto but she was saving it up to do it in her own bed at home. When we arrived her mama came out to the car and said, "You girls must be hungry," and took us in to the lunch table.

There was three-bean salad from cans packed with vinaigrette, pickle loaf on thin sliced white bread, American and Swiss cheese in slices, and antipasto from a jar sent directly from an uncle still living in New York City. "Deli food," her mama kept saying, "is the best food in the world." I nodded, chewing white bread and a slice of American cheese, the peanuts in my belly weighing me down like a mess of little stones. Mona picked at the pickle loaf and pushed her ankle up into my lap where her mother couldn't see. I choked on the white bread and broke out in a sweat.

Lee wore her hair pushed up like the whorls on scallop shells. She toasted mushrooms instead of marshmallows, and tried to persuade me of the value of cabbage and eggplant, but she cooked with no fat; everything tasted of safflower oil. I loved Lee but hated the cabbage—it seemed an anemic cousin of real greens—and I only got into the eggplant after Lee brought home a basketful insisting I help her cook it up for freezing.

"You got to get it to sweat out the poisons." She sliced the big purple fruits as she talked. "Salt it up so the bitter stuff will come off." She layered the salted slices between paper towels, changing the towels on the ones she'd cut up earlier. Some of her hair came loose and hung down past one ear. She looked like a mother in a Mary Cassatt painting, standing in her sunlit kitchen, sprinkling raw seasalt with one hand and pushing her hair back with the other.

I picked up an unsalted wedge of eggplant and sniffed it, rubbing the spongy mass between my thumbs. "Makes me think of what breadfruit must be like." I squeezed it down, and the flesh slowly shaped up again. "Smells like bread and feels like it's been baked. But after you salt it down, it's more like fried okra, all soft and sharp-smelling."

"Well, you like okra, don't you?" Lee wiped her grill with peanut oil and started dusting the drained eggplant slices with flour. Sweat shone on her neck under the scarf that tied up her hair in back.

"Oh yeah. You put enough cornmeal on it and fry it in bacon fat and I'll probably like most anything." I took the wedge of eggplant and rubbed it on the back of her neck.

"What are you doing?"

"Salting the eggplant." I followed the eggplant with my tongue, pulled up her T-shirt, and slowly ran the tough purple rind up to her small bare breasts. Lee started giggling, wiggling her ass, but not taking her hands out of the flour to stop me. I pulled down her shorts, picked up another dry slice and planted it against her navel, pressed with my fingers and slipped it down toward her pubic mound.

"Oh! Don't do that. Don't do that." She was breathing through her open mouth and her right hand was a knotted fist in the flour bowl. I laughed softly into her ear, and rocked her back so that she was leaning against me, her ass pressing into my cunt.

"Oh. Oh!" Lee shuddered and reached with her right hand to turn off the grill. With her left she reached behind her and pulled up on my shirt. Flour smeared over my sweaty midriff and sifted down on the floor. "You. You!" She was tugging at my jeans, a couple of slices of eggplant in one hand.

"I'll show you. Oh you!" We wrestled, eggplant breaking up between our navels. I got her shorts off, she got my jeans down. I dumped a whole plate of eggplant on her belly.

"You are just running salt, girl," I teased, and pushed slices up between her legs, while I licked one of her nipples and pinched the other between a folded slice of eggplant. She was laughing, her belly bouncing under me.

"I'm gonna make you eat all this," she yelled.

"Of course." I pushed eggplant out of the way and slipped two fingers between her labia. She was slicker than peanut oil. "But first we got to get the poison out."

"Oh you!" Her hips rose up into my hand. All her hair had come loose and was trailing in the flour. She wrapped one hand in my hair, the other around my left breast. "I'll cook you...just you wait. I'll cook you a meal to drive you crazy."

"Oh, honey." She tasted like frybread—thick, smoked, and fat-rich on my tongue. We ran sweat in puddles, while above us the salted eggplant pearled up in great clear drops of poison. When we finished, we gathered up all the eggplant on the floor and fried it in flour and crushed garlic. Lee poured canned tomatoes with basil and lemon on the hot slices and then pushed big bites onto my tongue with her fingers. It was delicious. I licked her fingers and fed her with my own hands. We never did get our clothes back on.

In South Carolina, in the seventh grade, we had studied nutrition. "Vitamin D," the teacher told us, "is paramount. Deny it to a young child and the result is the brain never develops properly." She had a twangy midwestern accent, grey hair, and a small brown mole on her left cheek. Everybody knew she hated teaching, hated her students, especially those of us in badly fitting worn-out dresses sucking bacon rinds and cutting our names in the desks with our uncle's old pocketknives. She would stand with a fingertip on her left ear, her thumb stroking that mole, while she looked at us with disgust she didn't bother to conceal.

"The children of the poor," she told us, "the children of the poor have a lack of brain tissue simply because they don't get the necessary vitamins at the proper age. It is a deficiency that cannot be made up when they are older." A stroke of her thumb and she turned her back.

I stood in the back of the room, my fingers wrapping my skull in horror. I imagined my soft brain slipping loosely in its cranial cavity shrunk by a lack of the necessary vitamins. How could I know if it wasn't too late? Mama always said that smart was the only way out. I thought of my cousins, big-headed, watery-eyed, and stupid. VITAMIN D! I became a compulsive consumer of vitamin D. Is it milk? We will drink milk, steal it if we must. *Mama, make salmon stew. It's cheap and full of vitamin D.* If we can't afford cream, then evaporated milk will do. One is as thick as the other. Sweet is expensive, but thick builds muscles in the brain. Feed me milk, feed me cream, feed me what I need to fight them.

Twenty years later the doctor sat me down to tell me the secrets of my body. He had, oddly, that identical gesture, one finger on the ear and the others curled to the cheek as if he were thinking all the time.

"Milk," he announced, "that's the problem, a mild allergy. Nothing to worry about. You'll take calcium and vitamin D supplements and stay away from milk products. No cream, no butterfat, stay away from cheese."

I started to grin, but he didn't notice. The finger on his ear was pointing to the brain. He had no sense of irony, and I didn't tell him why I laughed so much. I should have known. Milk or cornbread or black-eyed peas, there had to be a secret, something we would never understand until it was too late. My brain is fat and strong, ripe with years of vitamin D, but my belly is tender and hurts me in the night. I grinned into his confusion and chewed the pink and grey pills he gave me to help me recover from the damage milk had done me. What would I have to do, I wondered, to be able to eat pan gravy again?

When my stomach began to turn on me the last time, I made desperate attempts to compromise—wheat germ, brown rice, fresh vegetables and tamari. Whole wheat became a symbol for purity of intent, but hard brown bread does not pass easily. It sat in my stomach and clung to the honey deposits that seemed to be collecting between my tongue and breastbone. Lee told me I could be healthy if I drank a glass of hot water and lemon juice every morning. She chewed sunflower seeds and sesame seed candy made with molasses. I drank the hot water, but then I went up on the roof of the apartment building to read Carson McCullers, to eat Snickers bars and drink Dr. Pepper, imagining myself back in Uncle Lucius's Pontiac inhaling Moon Pies and R.C. Cola.

"Swallow it," Jay said. Her fingers were in my mouth, thick with the juice from between her legs. She was leaning forward, her full weight pressing me down. I swallowed, sucked between each knuckle, and swallowed again. Her other hand worked between us, pinching me but forcing the thick cream out of my cunt. She brought it up and pushed it into my mouth, took the hand I'd cleaned and smeared it again with her own musky gravy.

"Swallow it," she kept saying. "Swallow it all, suck my fingers, lick my palm." Her hips ground into me. She smeared it on my face until I closed my eyes under the sticky, strong-smelling mixture of her juice and mine. With my eyes closed, I licked and sucked until I was drunk on it, gasping until my lungs hurt with my hands digging into the muscles of her back. I was moaning and whining, shaking like a newborn puppy trying to get to its mama's tit.

Jay lifted a little off me. I opened stinging eyes to see her face, her intent and startling expression. I held my breath, waiting. I felt it before I understood it, and when I did understand I went on lying still under her, barely breathing. It burned me, ran all over my belly and legs. She put both hands down, brought them up, poured bitter yellow piss into my eyes, my ears, my shuddering mouth.

"Swallow it," she said again, but I held it in my mouth, pushed up against her and clawed her back with my nails. She whistled between her teeth. My hips jerked and rocked against her, making a

wet sucking sound. I pushed my face to hers, my lips to hers, and
forced my tongue into her mouth. I gripped her hard and rolled her
over, my tongue sliding across her teeth, the taste of all her juices
between us. I bit her lips and shoved her legs apart with my knee.
"Taste it," I hissed at her. "Swallow it." I ran my hands over her
body. My skin burned. She licked my face, growling deep in her throat.
I pushed both hands between her legs, my fingertips opened her and
my thumbs caught her clit under the soft sheath of its hood.

"Go on, go on," I insisted. Tears were running down her face.
I licked them. Her mouth was at my ear, her tongue trailing through
the sweat at my hairline. When she came her teeth clamped down
on my earlobe. I pulled but could not free myself. She was a thou-
sand miles away, rocking back and forth on my hand, the stink of
her all over us both. When her teeth freed my ear, I slumped. It felt
as if I had come with her. My thighs shook and my teeth ached. She
was mumbling with her eyes closed.

"Gonna bathe you," she whispered, "put you in a tub of hot lem-
onade. Drink it off you. Eat you for dinner." Her hands dug into my
shoulders, rolled me onto my back. She drew a long, deep breath
with her head back and then looked down at me, put one hand into
my cunt, and brought it up slick with my juice.

"Swallow it," Jay said. "Swallow it."

The year we held the great Southeastern Feminist Conference,
I was still following around behind Lee. She volunteered us to handle the food for the two hundred women that were expected. Lee
wanted us to serve "healthy food"—her vegetarian spaghetti sauce,
whole wheat pasta, and salad with cold fresh vegetables. Snacks would
be granola, fresh fruit, and peanut butter on seven-grain bread. For
breakfast she wanted me to cook grits in a twenty-quart pan, though
she wasn't sure margarine wouldn't be healthier than butter, and maybe
most people would just like granola anyway.

"They'll want donuts and coffee," I told her matter-of-factly. I had
a vision of myself standing in front of a hundred angry lesbians crying out for coffee and white sugar. Lee soothed me with kisses and
poppyseed cake made with gluten flour, assured me that it would be
fun to run the kitchen with her.

The week before the conference, Lee went from church to campus borrowing enormous pots, colanders, and baking trays. Ten flat
baking trays convinced her that the second dinner we had to cook
could be tofu lasagna with skim milk mozzarella and lots of chopped

carrots. I spent the week sitting in front of the pool table in Jay's apartment, peeling and slicing carrots, potatoes, onions, green and red peppers, leeks, tomatoes, and squash. The slices were dumped in ten-gallon garbage bags and stored in Jay's handy floor-model freezer. I put a tablecloth down on the pool table to protect the green felt and made mounds of vegetables over each pocket corner. Every mound cut down and transferred to a garbage bag was a victory. I was winning the war on vegetables until the committee Lee had scared up delivered another load.

I drank coffee and chopped carrots, ate a chicken pot pie and peeled potatoes, drank iced tea and sliced peppers. I peeled the onions but didn't slice them, dropped them into a big vat of cold water to keep. I found a meat cleaver on the back porch and used it to chop the zucchini and squash, pretending I was doing *karate* and breaking boards.

"Bite-sized," Lee told me as she ran through, "it should all be bite-sized." I wanted to bite her. I drank cold coffee and dropped tomatoes one at a time into boiling water to loosen their skins. There were supposed to be other women helping me, but only one showed up, and she went home after she got a rash from the tomatoes. I got out a beer, put the radio on loud, switching it back and forth from rock-and-roll to the country-and-western station and sang along as I chopped.

I kept working. The only food left in the apartment was vegetables. I wanted to have a pizza delivered but had no money. When I got hungry, I ate carrots on white bread with mayonnaise, slices of tomatoes between slices of raw squash, and leeks I dipped in a jar of low-sodium peanut butter. I threw up three times but kept working. Four hours before the first women were to arrive I took the last bushel basket of carrots out in the backyard and hid it under a tarp with the lawn mower. I laughed to myself as I did, swaying on rubbery legs. Lee drove up in a borrowed pickup truck with two women who'd come in from Atlanta and volunteered to help. One of them kept talking about the no-mucus diet as she loaded the truck. I went in the bathroom, threw up again, and then just sat on the tailgate in the sun while they finished up.

"You getting lazy, girl?" Lee teased me. "Better rev it up, we got cooking to do." I wiped my mouth and imagined burying her under a truckload of carrots. I felt like I had been drinking whiskey, but my stomach was empty and flat. The black top on the way out to the girl scout camp seemed to ripple and sway in the sunlight. Lee kept talking about the camp kitchen, the big black gas stove and the walk-in freezer.

"This is going to be fun." I didn't think so. The onions still had to be sliced. I got hysterical when someone picked up my knife. Lee was giggling with a woman I'd never seen before, the two of them talking about macrobiotic cooking while rinsing brown noodles. I got the meat cleaver and started chopping onions in big raw chunks. "Bite-sized," Lee called to me, in a cheerful voice.

"You want 'em bite-sized, you cut 'em," I told her, and went on chopping furiously.

It was late when we finally cleaned up. I hadn't been able to eat anything. The smell of the sauce had made me dizzy, and the scum that rinsed off the noodles looked iridescent and dangerous. My stomach curled up into a knot inside me, and I glowered at the women who came in and wanted hot water for tea. There were women sitting on the steps out on the deck, women around a campfire over near the water pump, naked women swimming out to the raft in the lake, and skinny, muscled women dancing continuously in the rec room. Lee had gone off with her new friend, the macrobiotic cook. I found a loaf of Wonderbread someone had left on the snack table, pulled out a slice and ate it in tiny bites.

"Want some?" It was one of the women from Atlanta. She held out a brown bag from which a bottle top protruded.

"It would make me sick."

"Naw," she grinned. "It's just a Yoo-hoo. I got a stash of them in a cooler. Got a bad stomach myself. Only thing it likes is chocolate soda and barbecue."

"Barbecue," I sighed. My mouth flooded with saliva. "I haven't made barbecue in years."

"You make beef ribs?" She sipped at her Yoo-hoo and sat down beside me.

"I have, but if you got the time to do slow pit cooking, pork's better." My stomach suddenly growled loudly, a grating, angry noise in the night.

"Girl," she laughed. "You still hungry?"

"Well, to tell you the truth, I couldn't eat any of that stuff." I was embarrassed.

My new friend giggled. "Neither did I. I had peanuts and Yoo-hoo for dinner myself." I laughed with her. "My name's Marty. You come up to Atlanta sometime, and we'll drive over to Marietta and get some of the best barbecue they make in the world."

"The best barbecue in the world?"

"Bar none." She handed me the bottle of Yoo-hoo.

"Can't be." I sipped a little. It was sweet and almost warm.

"You don't trust my judgment?" Someone opened the porch door, and I saw in the light that her face was relaxed, her blue eyes twinkling.

"I trust you. You didn't eat any of those damn noodles, did you? You're trustworthy, but you can't have the best barbecue in the world up near Atlanta, 'cause the best barbecue in the world is just a couple of miles down the Perry Highway."

"You say!"

"I do!"

We both laughed, and she slid her hip over close to mine. I shivered, and she put her arm around me. We talked, and I told her my name. It turned out we knew some of the same people. She had even been involved with a woman I hadn't seen since college. I was so tired I leaned my head on her shoulder. Marty rubbed my neck and told me a series of terribly dirty jokes until I started shaking more from giggling.

"Got to get you to bed," she started to pull me up. I took hold of her belt, leaned over, and kissed her. She kissed me. We sat back down and just kissed for a while. Her mouth was soft and tasted of sweet, watery chocolate.

"Uh huh," she said a few times, "uh huh."

"Uh huh," I giggled back.

"Oh yes, think we gonna have to check out this barbecue." Marty's hands were as soft as her mouth, and they slipped under the waistband of my jeans and hugged my belly. "You weren't fixed on having tofu lasagna tomorrow, were you?"

"Gonna break my heart to miss it, I can tell you." It was hard to talk with my lips pressed to hers. She licked my lips, the sides of my mouth, my cheek, my eyelids, and then put her lips up close to my ears.

"Oh, but think..." Her hands didn't stop moving, and I had to push myself back from her to keep from wetting my pants. "...Think about tomorrow afternoon when we come back from our little road trip hauling in all that barbecue, coleslaw, and hush puppies. We gonna make so many friends around here." She paused. "They do make hush puppies at this place, don't they?"

"Of course. If we get there early enough, we might even pick up some blackberry cobbler at this truck stop I know." My stomach rumbled again loudly.

"I don't think you been eating right," Marty giggled. "Gonna have to feed you some healthy food, girl, some *healthy* food."

Jay does *karate*, does it religiously, going to class four days in a week and working out at the gym every other day. Her muscles are hard and long. She is so tall people are always making jokes about "the weather up there." I call her *Shorty* or *Tall* to tease her, and *Sugar Hips* when I want to make her mad. Her hips are wide and full, though her legs are long and stringy.

"Lucky I got big feet," she jokes sometimes, "or I'd fall over every time I stopped to stand still."

Jay is always hungry, always. She keeps a bag of nuts in her backpack, dried fruit sealed in cellophane in a bowl on her dresser, snackpacks of crackers and cheese in her locker at the gym. When we go out to the women's bar, she drinks one beer in three hours but eats half a dozen packages of smoked almonds. Her last girlfriend was Italian. She used to serve Jay big batches of pasta with homemade sausage marinara.

"I need carbohydrates," Jay insists, eating slices of potato bread smeared with sweet butter. I cook grits for her, with melted butter and cheese, fry slabs of cured ham I get from a butcher who swears it has no nitrates. She won't eat eggs, won't eat shrimp or oysters, but she loves catfish pan-fried in a batter of cornmeal and finely chopped onions. Coffee makes her irritable. Chocolate makes her horny. When my period is coming and I get that flushed heat feeling in my insides, I bake her tollhouse cookies, serve them with a cup of coffee and a blush. She looks at me over the rim of the cup, sips slowly, and eats her cookies with one hand, the other hooked in her jeans by her thumb. A muscle jumps in her cheek, and her eyes are full of tiny lights.

"You hungry, honey?" she purrs. She stretches like a big cat, puts her bare foot up, and uses her toes to lift my blouse. "You want something sweet?" Her toes are cold. I shiver and keep my gaze on her eyes. She leans forward and cups her hands around my face. "What you hungry for, girl, huh? You tell me. You tell mama exactly what you want."

Her name was Victoria, and she lived alone. She cut her hair into a soft cloud of curls and wore white blouses with buttoned-down collars. I saw her all the time at the bookstore, climbing out of her baby blue VW with a big leather book bag and a cane in her left hand. There were pictures up on the wall at the back of the store. Every one of them showed her sitting on or standing by a horse, the reins loose in her hand and her eyes focused far off. The riding hat hid her curls. The jacket pushed her breasts down but emphasized her hips. She had a ribbon pinned to the coat. A little card beneath the pictures identified her as the steeplechase champion of the southern division. In one picture she was jumping. Her hat was gone, her hair blown back, and the horse's legs stretched high above the ground. Her teeth shone white and perfect, and she looked as fierce as a bobcat going for prey. Looking at the pictures made me hurt. She came in once while I was standing in front of them and gave me a quick, wry grin.

"You ride?" Her cane made a hollow thumping sound on the floor. I didn't look at it.

"For fun, once or twice with a girlfriend." Her eyes were enormous and as black as her hair. Her face looked thinner than it had in the pictures, her neck longer. She grimaced and leaned on the cane. Under her tan she looked pale. She shrugged.

"I miss it myself." She said it in a matter-of-fact tone, but her eyes glittered. I looked up at the pictures again.

"I'll bet." I blushed, and looked back at her uncomfortably.

"Odds are I'll ride again." Her jeans bulged around the knee brace. "But not jump, and I did love jumping. Always felt like I was at war with the ground, allied with the sky, trying to stay up in the air." She grinned wide, and a faint white scar showed at the corner of her mouth.

"Where you from?" I could feel the heat in my face but ignored it.

"Virginia." Her eyes focused on my jacket, the backpack hanging from my arm, and down to where I had my left hip pushed out, my weight on my right foot. "Haven't been there for a while, though." She looked away, looked tired and sad. What I wanted in that moment I will never be able to explain—to feed her or make love to her or just lighten the shadows under her eyes—all that, all that and more.

"You ever eat any Red Velvet Cake?" I licked my lips and shifted my weight so that I wasn't leaning to the side. I looked into her eyes.

"Red Velvet Cake?" Her eyes were friendly, soft, black as the deepest part of the night.

"It's a dessert my sister and I used to bake, unhealthy as sin and twice as delicious. Made up with chocolate, buttermilk, vinegar and baking soda, and a little bottle of that poisonous red dye number two. Tastes like nothing you've ever had."

"You got to put the dye in it?"

"Uh huh," I nodded, "wouldn't be right without it."

"Must look deadly."

"But tastes good. It's about time I baked one. You come to dinner at my place, tell me about riding, and I'll cook you up one." She shifted, leaned back, and half-sat on a table full of magazines. She looked me up and down again, her grin coming and going with her glance.

"What else would you cook?"

"Fried okra maybe, fried crisp, breaded with cornmeal. Those big beefsteak tomatoes are at their peak right now. Could just serve them in slices with pepper, but I've seen some green ones, too, and those I could fry in flour with the okra. Have to have white corn, of course, this time of the year. Pinto beans would be too heavy, but snap beans would be nice. A little milk gravy to go with it all. You like fried chicken?"

"Where you from?"

"South Carolina, a long time ago."

"You mama teach you to cook?"

"My mama and my aunts." I put my thumbs in my belt and tried to look sure of myself. Would she like biscuits or cornbread, pork or beef or chicken?

"I'm kind of a vegetarian." She sighed when she said it, and her eyes looked sad.

"Eat fish?" I was thinking quickly. She nodded. I smiled wide.

"Ever eat any crawfish pan-fried in salt and Louisiana hot sauce?"

"You got to boil them first." Her face was shining, and she was bouncing her cane on the hardwood floor.

"Oh yeah, 'course, with the right spices."

"Sweet Bleeding Jesus," her face was flushed. She licked her lips. "I haven't eaten anything like that in, oh, so long."

"Oh." My thighs felt hot, rubbing on the seams of my jeans. She was beautiful, Victoria in her black cloud of curls. "Oh, girl," I whispered. I leaned toward her. I put my hand on her wrist above the cane, squeezed.

"Let me feed you," I told her. "Girl . . . girl, you should just let me feed you what you really need."

I've been dreaming lately that I throw a dinner party, inviting all the women in my life. They come in with their own dishes. Marty brings barbecue carried all the way fom Marietta. Jay drags in a whole side of beef and gets a bunch of swaggering whiskey-sipping butch types to help her dig a hole in the backyard. They show off for each other, breaking up stones to line the firepit. Lee watches them from the porch, giggling at me and punching down a great mound of dough for the oatmeal wheat bread she'd promised to bake. Women whose names I can't remember bring in bowls of pasta salad, smoked salmon, and jello with tangerine slices. Everybody is feeding each other, exclaiming over recipes and gravies, introducing themselves and telling stories about great meals they've eaten. My mama is in the kitchen salting a vat of greens. Two of my aunts are arguing over whether to make little baking powder biscuits or big buttermilk hogsheads. Another steps around them to slide an iron skillet full of cornbread in the oven. Pinto beans with onions are bubbling on the stove. Children run through sucking fatback rinds. My uncles are on the porch telling stories and knocking glass bottles together when they laugh.

I walk back and forth from the porch to the kitchen, being hugged and kissed and stroked by everyone I pass. For the first time in my life I am not hungry, but everybody insists I have a little taste. I burp like a baby on her mama's shoulder. My stomach is full, relaxed, happy, and the taste of pan gravy is in my mouth. I can't stop grinning. The dream goes on and on, and through it all I hug myself and smile.

LUPUS

"You don't get home often enough."

It is August and high summer has fattened all the trees on Old Henderson Road, dried the road to powder and grey loose loam, coating the myrtle and dogwood trees with a flat white alkali stain. Temple sits on her porch while her oldest girl rinses her hairpins in a tub of bleach and spring water. Off in the yard, the dogs raise a dust cloud. I wipe sweat off my mouth and drink tea like I never left home.

Temple slides her palms on the worn porch step, flat and smooth under her hands, back and forth. We watch a long green trailer turn the corner, shear the leaves on the myrtle, just miss the leaning porch, the poplar, the young dogwood.

"That would have done it," Temple laughs softly, open-mouthed and happy. "I could have put in the new plumbing this year 'stead of next. Anything that big's got to be insured."

I nod, scratch chigger bites on my ankles, unable to relax to pissing in the weeds, hoping that trailer comes back and pays for more than the plumbing. She married late, Cousin Temple did, married late and well—a steady boy, one of those Roberts from Ashville, a lean, freckled, still boy, as steady as she was and as quiet,

---

Lupus: Any of various skin diseases; especially a chronic tuberculous disease of the skin or mucous membranes; a particularly dangerous disease of metabolical origin—incurable but sometimes controlled by steroid drugs—which exhausts the energies of its victims and necessitates an extremely careful and restricted life.

Lupus: A wolf, from 'eating into the substance of'; cancer.

a good son who loved his mother and never ran around like the other boys all the other cousins married early.

Temple rolls a little hair between two fingers and turns her red-tan face up into the sun slanting past the porch beams. This house, yard, dirt road, myrtle trees, kudzu holding the screens on the windows—none of it would stand up to a Northern winter, a Yankee tax assessor, or an estate sale. But it puts Temple outside them, a property owner, something none of the rest of the family can imagine becoming. Temple has been an outsider all her life, though living on her own since her mama left her with her own mother when Temple was barely seven—a quiet red-faced seven as she is now a quiet red-faced woman whose hair shows grey where it lays close to her skull.

"You were a bean when you were a girl," Temple tells me, "a string bean, and your sister was a butter bean. Your mama was a stretch of stringy pork, and together you didn't make a decent Sunday dinner."

When Temple laughs, her head goes back. Her long red hair shakes out, and all the grey she has so skillfully tried to hide flows loose and flashes at me, silver and white. "Temple," I tell her, "you're finally getting old."

"Bullshit," she flares. "And apple butter. I'm just more woman than the men in this town can handle. And I've more left to me than most people get to start out." Then she smiles, oh she smiles! The skin around her mouth that's aged so dry and tight flushes and fills like the grin on a mewling baby. But her teeth slip loose, and her hand flies up to hide the wolf grin.

"Goddamn," she sighs. Her daughter doesn't look up. Temple's hand caresses her porch, strokes the soft, worn wood like the lover she barely remembers. "It an't Robert, you know, but it is, I'd swear. All I have of him anyway. Nights, I seem to hear him breathing, but it's the walls. They sweat so, they smell just the way he did. And I got to where I don't care if I'm crazy. I talk to this house like it was him."

Somehow it is. There was an army insurance policy, a thousand-dollar burial, and a four-thousand-dollar mortgage, plus two more for the plumbing which never worked anyway. In the North, it would have bought nothing; in Ashville only a little more; but out here

off Old Henderson Road in 1959 it was an estate for three or-
phans and a red-headed woman suddenly going grey.

"Lupus," she says, "it was Lupus." An old story I have heard many
times these twenty-five years. Temple scratches herself, and spits,
angry now as she was angry then. "Damn doctors, damn hospi-
tals, never said what else. Lupus, you know, kills slow, takes a
long time—years. But Robert, Lord, Robert sank into that bed.
He died so fast. Weeks seemed like no time. He just melted away."

Maryat stirs her hairpins. Claire brings a pitcher of tea to the door.
I wipe my mouth again, saying nothing, watching the sweat shine
on Temple's cheeks. When I was a child and slept in her bed,
I would lie awake and watch the line—eyelids to cheekbones to
mouth. Never touched it, never once reached out to touch her
cheekbone, though I dreamed of pulling her into my neck, sucking
her throat, and licking her eyes. Now I curl my fingers around
my hipbones, hug myself, and don't quite reach out to her trembling hands.

"You never saw the store, did you?" Little flecks of broken woodgrain
pull up under Temple's fingernails. "Your mama wouldn't bring
you girls around. Hell, your mama thought you girls were meant
to be special, wasn't gonna carry you around to no honky-tonk
roadhouse." She reaches for me, touching my sun-warmed thigh.

"But it wasn't like that, not really. The store was across from the high
school and clean as a dried peach pit. Scrubbed hollow, hell,
I scrubbed me raw. We had pinball machines, and a candy counter,
Coke coolers, chip racks, and billiards. No liquor 'cept for Robert's
beer in the back cooler."

"But we lost it, of course. We lost everything."

Temple pauses, pulls at her tea and frowns. "Hard to remember all
that, hard times and craziness. I was crazy, you know, oh yes.
We lost the store, the car, even the baby's bed—all those weeks
with Robert lying still, breathing like a train going up a hill. All
that slow, crazy time, and me crazy. Me just out of my head. I
was howling at Granny, screaming at the girls, tearing at myself.
Hated myself, like I'd done it, like I'd brought it on him. Nobody in his family had it, but Granny said we'd had a cousin
with it, so maybe it had come through me."

"It was important then, how it had come on us. Later I didn't care, but then it was like that was the only thing that mattered."

Dust drifts down in the sunlight. Another truck turns the corner and shakes the porch. It's a shortcut, this road and Temple's lot. Truckers come through and wave. Temple ignores them, slaps her porch, watches the dirty paint flake down. The dogs in the yard, tied off to a tree, howl and kick and lie down again, panting in the heat.

"I got mustard grass, you know, and yellow nettles. Grow 'em 'cause it makes people mad, 'cause an't nobody can tell me anything. It keeps people away, makes sure no one touches what's mine."

They still have fireflies in Greenville, and green tree frogs, katydids, and rock-sucking worms. The muscadines still hang in sheets off the trees behind Old Henderson Road. Once every few years, Temple takes up with some traveling man, someone she can't see staying around. She wants nobody permanent now, not after Robert and the girls, that first baby, everybody she ever loved.

"Temple's nothing but trouble," the cousins claim. They complain of her life, her girls. "Hard-assed, cold-hearted woman." Everybody agrees. "Thinks more of that ratty-walled house than her family, thinks more of herself than a woman should."

Off Old Henderson Road, the porches tilt. The paint chips off. Temple's bathroom is still out back of the pines. She has the cousins come over to prop the windows, wire back the roof where the slats are sliding down. Where the paint has gone, the wood stays bare and rain-marked. She won't paint again, says it will just flake off in the heat.

Kids come over from West Greenville, drive their pickups right up on the grass, hide behind the dead vines that shield the shed out back; stare in where Temple stores broken chairs, empty boxes, an extra bed. They giggle a lot, smoke dope, and occasionally fall through the rotten boards.

You gonna pay for that you white-eyed sonofabitch!

Temple threatens to pen that shed for chickens, set traps, loose the dogs. All she really does is talk to the uncles real loud on the phone.

Come up here and shoot me a few of these bastards!

Sometimes she doesn't bother to dial. Sometimes she doesn't bother to roll over or get up, lies in bed for a day, her face set and angry so the girls know to stay away. Gets up thinner but quiet. Goes back to work as the crossing guard at Greenville South-East, the only work she's had since Robert died.

"You ever read that Flannery O'Connor? I got the book from Macon a few years back. Heard she'd had the Lupus, thought it might be in there, but God knows it an't. You read that crazy woman? Made me think people're worse than I thought, and I thought bad enough. But the worst was some of it made me laugh and then made me 'shamed. Thinking, what kind of woman laughs at such troubles? Babies drowning themselves for Jesus, preachers and old ladies that get their whole families shot dead 'cause they forgot the right highway."

Flat, flat, her hand, her face, the sunlight on the porch. Temple's memory of a boy dead now twenty-five years. "I'd hate to think it was the Lupus."

"Get her to think of something else," Mama asked me. "People say she's going crazy out on that old porch."

Nobody really knows Temple. The women smile about her, say, *Lord God, but she loved that man.* Everybody says it's a pity, how she sits, how she doesn't get on with her life, take another husband, have another child, plant zinnias or baby's breath and go on. Go on.

I sit on Temple's porch and drink coffee, drink tea when the morning heats up, talk to her of New York and California, of cities she's never seen. I watch how she laughs, her red hair swinging from side to side, bringing the grey and white to the surface, bringing out the shadows and wrinkles under her eyes.

"How can you live in a city? All those pictures like to make my heart hurt. I could smell it—hot concrete, tar, and piss. No green for miles. No color a'tall. Lord, where's the life in it?"

I tell her about the color of night, the lights on the bridges, the hot shine in the women's eyes, the cold glare of metal moving fast. I tell her about the cold winter light shining on flat stacks of slate, hanging over the New Jersey highways, the cars growling rock music out their vents—how tight the people wear their clothes, how tall the buildings, how sweet the dawn after you do not sleep for days.

The silence answers me. I wipe my fingertips on the porch, smell myrtle and crushed onion through the dust of passing trucks, watch Claire cross the yard, how she swings her arms and throws back her head, her white face with the black eyebrows etched as high and fierce as crows across the highway. I have not been this still in years, have not heard my own heart when I was not shadowed by full dark and bourbon, not looked into a face that mirrored mine as Temple's does—bone to bone, ancient grief to daily rage.

"How do you do it?" I ask her. "How do you live this far from the rest of the world?"

"What do I need the world for?" Temple laughs at me. "Besides I got sugar, just like Granny. Came on two years ago, and 'pressure, they say, though I an't checking. What good is it to know you gonna die sooner than later? It makes me think the world's too damn close on me anyway."

"Claire, honey, pour me another glass of tea."

Claire, the wire child, thin as the poplar on the corner, pale as the birch peeling in the backyard, brings the jug in two hands and smiles at me. The little reddish-brown nodules on her shoulders could be freckles but are not. The flush under Temple's skin deepens, and her hands start to shake on the glass. She is seeing what I am watching—Claire's smile and those deadly little warts.

"You know, a lot of famous people died of the Lupus. But then people have it for years and never die, or at least, don't die of just that." She sighs, rolls the ragged ends of her hair between fingers suddenly flushed pink.

"You know what I did?" She looks away, away from me, away from her daughter, away from the dogs who paw restlessly at the bare patches near the trees. "I let them take his body. Told them to go ahead, do anything they had to. When it came down to it, I said, just tell me what it was. The girls, of course, I was thinking of the girls. And they took him, did their stuff to him, things I can't even imagine. I don't think, in the end, we buried more than the frame of him."

Temple's hands shake, her tea spills over the splintered boards of the porch. Leaning forward makes her face go a deeper red. "Doctors, like lawyers you know, they don't hurry."

"I thought it would be a while, weeks maybe, even months. But Lord, years! I never thought they'd take years, and then tell me nothing. Just the Lupus, 'cause of the spots and the strangling. Lupus like with Claire or that cousin I don't know that I really believe ever existed. But hell, they didn't really know what killed him. Lupus kills slow, and Robert died fast."

"Sometimes, sometimes, I dream sometimes, oh God!" Temple rocks her head back and forth, casts a glance at her daughters and looks quickly away, speaking in a whisper that does not carry to where they sit. "I dream sometimes I lead the children out in front of a big old semi, a row of hearses following easy as you please, all their daddies nodding at me as they're mowed down!"

She shakes her head, shakes her shoulders, her whole torso following, the pink in her cheeks going brighter than sunburn.

"But, sometimes, too, I dream I am alone, walking through Greenville as it burns, the sparks coming down on my neck but nothing burning me. No one sees me. They come out and throw water and yell. I just walk through and grin. Imagine the kind of woman I am to take pleasure in that kind of thing!"

Imagine the kind of woman she is, Temple on her porch with the paint flaking down. Temple with her hands still on her knees, ridged and knobby, the veins blue-purple and high. Her face a permanent red-tan flush. Her daughters going in and out, slowly, carefully, the deadly warts on the pale skin of their necks and calves burning her eyes.

Imagine what kind of a woman sits still, safe in her own mind, slow as myrtle leaves turning. Sugar thickening the blood in her veins, pressure pinking her skin. Wanting nothing more than new plumbing and her daughters' slow movement forward, alive. Some man to come along now and then, never quite as real as the man who lives behind her eyes.

Temple writes me once a year, a letter that lists who's died, who's been born, a letter that ends with a reminder of who she is. She is my favorite cousin, after me the most remarkable, the one who lived with us the year I was seven, the year mama almost died, the year she first had cancer and I fell in love with the very idea of red-headed women.

"Do you hear from Temple?" Mama always asks me. "She say anything about the girls? Heard from Dot that Maryat was planning on getting married and Claire wasn't doing very well at all."

Every year I do not go home, it hurts me. I think of Temple, the year I was seven and she was eighteen; the year I was eleven and she lost her lover; the year she lost her teeth and her baby girl; the years I realized she would never be mine.

"Do you hear from Temple?" My mama, my cousins, my aunts always ask. I am the one she writes to, and if I have not heard from her then no one has. Sometimes I do not answer, I fall into Temple's white-eyed memories, the silence of her flushed cheeks, her thin face and hot eyes. The wolf in my neck bares his teeth, stretches, lays one paw on the other, dreaming of fire and sparks raining down, myrtle leaves blackening in the heat. I fight him with my love for Temple, hug to myself the warmth and stillness of her porch, the certainty that she does not fear the wolf in her, the wolf who hides his teeth but watches, watches out of her eyes.